BAD MAN'S TRAIL

Center Point
Large Print

This Large Print Book carries the
Seal of Approval of N.A.V.H.

BAD MAN'S TRAIL

ELI COLTER

Center Point Large Print
Thorndike, Maine

This Center Point Large Print edition
is published in the year 2023 by arrangement with
Golden West Inc.

Originally published in the US by A. H. King.

The text of this Large Print edition is unabridged.
In other aspects, this book may vary
from the original edition.
Printed in the United States of America
on permanent paper sourced using
environmentally responsible foresting methods.
Set in 16-point Times New Roman type.

ISBN 978-1-63808-734-2 (hardcover)
ISBN 978-1-63808-738-0 (paperback)

The Library of Congress has cataloged this record
under Library of Congress Control Number: 2023930237

CONTENTS

Prologue

Moving slowly, with a kind of deliberate majesty, along a shaded veranda floor, across a close-clipped lawn or up a stone wall, the great mottled grey-green-and-black terrestrial gastropod leaves behind him a narrow band of glittering web, and all who look may see by what route he has passed. So man. Man, moving along the surface of the world, leaves behind him a band of web, a mere narrow thread, woven of thoughts, desires, dreams, passions, inhibitions and deeds. Man and gastropod differ in this; the gastropod's thread is silver, always, while man's is many hued.

Over the earth they ray, the threads man leaves; and all who look may see by what route he has passed, by what dreams he has builded, by what passions he has been driven and by what deeds he is remembered.

Here lies a thread tinted the hot smouldering purple of passion. Yonder winds another shaded leaden grey with grief. And yet another, and another. Count them, tabulate their colors. Their faintest tones are easily distinguished. Dun with despair, rose-red with romance, chrome yellow with cowardice, black with evil, softly blue with the valiancy of spirit, green with the eroding verdigris of bitterness, sober brown with steady sturdy living. Over here one shows, a hardier thread, of bronze, seasoned by much exposure to the sun. And lastly there becomes apparent a thread that is crystal clear with the untouched chastity of youth; a thread destined to become shaded, as shaded as the rainbow, as the different currents of life cast upon it the stain of their varying influences.

At a given hour of destiny all these threads meet and pass, cross and weave, forming patterns marvelous and strange. What an enormous amount of interest there would be for the observer to take one or two of those threads at the head, and follow them through their twisting and winding, watching the patterns as they began to form, intermingle and blend, to see at last the full-fashioned polychrome tapestry.

Thus, then, one has found the first thread of a designated section; the brown thread of steady sturdy living. To the observer the threads become fascinating only when they begin to weave. One picks up the brown thread where it first begins to weave with the thread that is green with the verdigris of old bitterness long remembered. The brown thread leads to a high and heavy door, the front entrance to an unpretentious solid old mansion.

Chapter I

THE SINISTER CALL

The great door stood closed, like a forbidding portal to some undivinable labyrinthian retreat. It was decorated by an iron knocker fitted with a tumbler which dropped a tongue upon a deep-toned brass gong. The gong clanged three times in rapid succession. Its mellow brazen tones were fused into a rumble as the huge knocker responded to the grip of an importunate hand. The imperative sound charged down the wide hallway, ricocheted back and forth from wall to wall, to burst finally, urgently, into the room opening off the end of the hallway beyond the carved marble staircase. The room was the private sanctum of the master of the house, Bruce Taight, many times a millionaire, and as many times a man.

Sitting before his desk, his head cocked sidewise in study, Taight roused himself and raised his eyes in sudden interest at the clang of the gong. He heard the fragmentary interchange of voices; then silence, followed by a rap on his door.

"It's Mr Costa, sir," said the butler.

"Yeh. Come on in, Costa." Taight straightened

in his chair and got to his feet as the door swung open. "I've been waiting for you to show up."

Satisfaction smoothed the heavy anxiety on his face as he advanced with outstretched hand.

The man who had entered the room was slightly under medium height, slimly built and immaculately dressed. His thick smooth hair was an ordinary light brown in tone. His mild hazel eyes matched it exactly in color. His close-cropped mustache and short blunt beard were grey enough to place, though not too definitely, his fifty-odd years.

After a cursory view of the commonplace picture he presented, you might label him offhand "doctor," and find your interest in him entirely dissipated. But if you were one of those who read between the bold print and seek the water-mark, you would look again at the mild hazel eyes. And you would discover that the expressionless cast of them, which at first you had taken to be listless indolence, was in reality the motionless alertness of a super intellect eternally on guard. Beyond that you could not read.

Years gone, Earle Costa stood and looked down upon the dead face of his brother, Guido Costa. Those two, strangers and aliens to the rest of their kin, had been one in thought, bound by affection of fiery intenseness peculiar to the Latin blood. Earle Costa, shaken by a blast of rage and grief, had bent over that still face and spoken as though Guido were alive, had sworn vengeance upon his brother's murderer, had vowed that he himself would bring that murderer to account as he himself conceived the account to be just.

Long years between had left no trace upon Earle Costa, externally. The thick light hair had as yet to show its first strand of grey. The grey in beard and mustache was largely camouflaged by the lightness of his complexion, discounted by the un-grey hair. There was not upon the surface any evidence of the corroding acid of bitterness within. Yet, the passing of time had only deepened its burning power over him. Those who knew Earle Costa, mild and quiet, unostentatiously brilliant in his profession, would have been confounded to learn that, underneath that placid exterior there seethed a pent malignity ready to burst forth and destroy another man or any member of that man's immediate family, the moment they could be found. That he had failed through all the intervening years to get trace of Guido's murderer or that murderer's kin had but served to inflame his determination that a day of reckoning should be brought to pass, sometime, somewhere.

Bruce Taight, half a head taller, big, bluff and blunt, looked into Costa's unreadable eyes with a grin. He liked Earle Costa tremendously.

"What do you want now?" Costa demanded, with some amusement. "Want to drag me on another fishing trip and give the mosquitos a banquet?"

"Wrong the first guess," Taight returned, his grin fading. "Sit down, Earle. I called you in a professional capacity, this time."

"Oh." Costa took the chair Taight indicated, as the big man went back around his desk and dropped into a seat before it. He drew from his pocket a vile pipe and began packing the bowl with Turkish leaf from a small leather pouch. The amusement was still in his voice. "What's the matter, Bruce? Somebody trying to gyp you out of a couple million?"

"Worse than that." Taight frowned, laid a hand on a small package on the desk in front of him, and raised a sudden sharp glance to Costa's face. "I have received a birthday present."

Costa paused in the act of lighting his pipe, wondering if he had heard right. "Did you say a birthday present? And you sent for me?" He eyed Taight with penetrating calculation, and added dryly; "I might ask, *which* professional capacity?"

Taight frowned more deeply than before. "Sounds like I was ready for the psychopathic ward, does it? I get a birthday present and I send for the most brilliant detective that ever posed as a doctor. But take a look at the present before you express any opinions on my mental condition. I just got back from Florida yesterday, and I found this waiting for me. It came in the afternoon mail, about two hours before I arrived. In spite of the crazy name on it, I knew by the address and postmark that it was meant for me, so I opened it. Take a look at it."

He shoved across the desk the package he had been fingering. Costa picked it up and turned it over in his hands. Taight had returned it to its original wrapping. It was addressed in scrawling penmanship to Mr Articulo Mortis. The street number was that of Taight's New York home address. Costa's eyes lingered for a moment over the odd-sounding name, then passed on without any seeming interest. He removed the wrapping paper to find within it a small cloth-bound book a great deal the worse for wear, thumbed and soiled and not a little tattered. It bore the terse title Hymn Book. Costa flipped back the cover to glance at the flyleaf. Penned in the same scrawling chirography as that addressing the package were the words:

"Just a little birthday gift from your old
friend L. S.
For old time's sake."

Costa studied the page for a moment, then pointed to the pen-drawn symbol just below the initials in the inscription. "What's that. Looks like a crude drawing of one of these old iron kettles."

"It is. You've heard me speak of my rancher friend out in Montana. That is the brand of his ranch, the Iron Kettle."

"I see. What was there about it that caused you to send for me, outside of the fact that it bears your address but not your name?"

"Everything," Taight answered grimly. "In the first place, why that crazy name? In the second place, the writing on the wrapper and flyleaf is not his. In the third place, he never sent me a birthday present before, and I've known him for twenty-five years. If he'd ever gone so far off his normal track as to send me a birthday present, he'd have been more likely to inscribe something like—'Here you've got away with another year, you old highbinder; why in hell don't you kick off?' And he might have scribbled 'Lew' after it, but he never would have signed 'your old friend L. S.' " Taight went silent, staring at the book, and Costa prodded him on.

"Yes? Is that all?"

"It is not! Lew never had a hymn book in his house. Neither of us has ever been religious. Neither of us can sing, don't know one note from the other. And my birthday is seven months distant, and Lew knows it. Everything concerning that book is unnatural. It seems to me intentionally so. As though it were sent for the express purpose of arousing my suspicion and demanding my investigation. That's why I called you. You can begin thinking where I left off."

Costa made no reply. He sat motionless, puffing indolently at his pipe, gazing at the flyleaf and its inscription. Then he began idly turning the leaves of the book, slowly, careful not to miss a single one, and his slim fingers slipped over each surface in an almost indetectible smoothing motion, as though he were pressing each page down into place. Taight watched patiently.

Leaf by leaf Costa turned on, till he came to a place somewhat beyond the middle of the book. There he stopped, eyeing the page spread before him. Suddenly he held it up for Taight's inspection.

"See anything there, Bruce?" he asked.

Taight's eyes narrowed in close scrutiny. An old and well-known hymn occupied the page. The title, in heavy blackface type, stood in orderly dignity above music and stanzas: *My Faith Looks Up to Thee.* But nothing noteworthy was visible to Taight's gaze save that at the end of the title was drawn another facsimile of the Iron Kettle brand. Costa extended the book toward him. Taight took the hymnal and ran his fingers over the page, as he had seen the detective do. A slight irregular roughness attracted his attention. He brought the book closer to his eyes.

Less schooled in the art of dissembling, less habituated to concealing his emotions, than Costa, the millionaire uttered an exclamation of surprise. Scattered around over the page were numerous pinholes, made apparently with no intent or design. The roughness caused by the holes had carried instant meaning to Costa's sensitive fingers. Taight returned the book to the detective, his puzzled frown deepening.

"But I don't see how those pinholes can mean anything, Earle."

Again Costa made no reply. His mild hazel eyes continued to dwell on the perforated page. He bent back the remainder of the leaves, so that the page stood out by itself, held the book up against the light, rose abruptly, drew a fine-pointed pencil from his pocket and stepped to the nearest window. He pushed the curtain aside and, with the remainder of the leaves still bent back, he laid against the pane the pin-pricked sheet bearing the Iron Kettle brand. Like a minute spot of dim light each hole showed up clearly on the darker blur of the paper. With the sharp pencil point Costa carefully imprinted a black dot on each small hole. Then he returned to his chair.

From another pocket he took a blank sheet of note paper and braced it upon the opposite side of the book, holding the volume now spread flat open. Upon the note paper he copied the verses of the hymn. Then, beginning at the top of the page, one by one, at the right of the verses he had written down, he jotted the letters over which the pinholes had been made. He worked perhaps for ten minutes in utter silence. Then having worked to a conclusion the problem the page presented, the detective laid the sheet of note paper upon the open face of the book and passed the two articles across to Taight.

"There's your answer, Bruce. I thought you knew the meaning of the Latin phrase camouflaged as a name on the wrapper. I really thought that that had been the thing which impelled you to call me, which had aroused your suspicions. On the face of it, it looks decidedly sinister. But look it over before I say any more. I want to get your reaction to it. You know your friend well enough to be able to judge whether or not he is the type of man to become unduly alarmed."

Taight reached eagerly for the book and note paper, startled. Costa added slowly;

"It's quite clear, I believe, that the two dots which are placed one above the other in the second verse of the first stanza are meant to indicate that, in decoding the message, he wanted you to double the letter designated. I did so, and my supposition proves itself."

Taight but half heard him. The startled sense with which he had received Costa's words was intensified by what he saw on the sheet. At first he had been inclined to consider the whole thing as a jest. But this was no jest. This was what he read:

MR ARTICULO MORTIS . . . from the Latin phrase *in articulo mortis.* Meaning *at the point of death.*

MY FAITH LOOKS UP TO THEE

MY FAITH LOOKS UP TO THEE,
THOU LAMB OF CALVARY,
SAVIOR DIVINE.
NOW HEAR ME WHILE I PRAY, TAKE
ALL MY GUILT AWAY,
O, LET ME FROM THIS DAY BE
WHOLLY THINE.
MAY THY RICH GRACE IMPART
STRENGTH TO MY FAINTING
HEART,
MY ZEAL INSPIRE.
AS THOU HAST DIED FOR ME, O,
MAY MY LOVE FOR THEE,
PURE, WARM AND CHANGELESS
BE—A LIVING FIRE.
WHILE LIFE'S DARK MAZE I
TREAD AND GRIEFS AROUND ME
SPREAD, BE THOU MY GUIDE:
BID DARKNESS TURN TO DAY, WIPE

SORROW'S TEARS AWAY,
NOR EVER LET ME STRAY FROM
THEE ASIDE.
WHEN ENDS LIFE'S TRANSIENT
DREAM, WHEN DEATH'S COLD
SULLEN STREAM
SHALL O'ER ME ROLL:
BLEST SAVIOR THEN IN LOVE,
FEAR AND DISTRUST REMOVE,
O BEAR ME SAFE ABOVE—A
RANSOMED SOUL.

MYSTERYSADLESTHERANCHDAMN
EDUGLYOUTFITSOS

Mystery saddles the ranch.
Damned ugly outfit. S.O.S.

He studied the page with its sinister message for some time. Finally he spoke, bluntly.

"That *is* like him. No, he isn't a man to be unduly alarmed. Something is wrong at the Iron Kettle. Damned wrong! I'm having my private car switched onto the next train bound for the West." Taight literally jumped to his feet and began pacing excitedly back and forth between his desk and the window. For a moment the astonishing communication pricked into that page by a pin had, by its very unexpectedness and sinister tone, served to stun Taight into dumb-ness. But now that he had grasped its serious significance, his excited concern rose in a surge of desire for action.

"Oh, hold on a minute." Costa looked up at him with cool inexpressive eyes and an impassive countenance, lounging in his chair with a settled ease that somehow was more eloquent of racing thought and alert perception than all of Taight's pacing and expletory words. "That wouldn't do. And getting excited won't do. Sit down, Bruce, and give me your attention. What is this man's name?"

"Sudler, Lew Sudler."

"What kind of man is he?"

"Oh, all kinds of man." Taight paused in his pacing, took a step toward his chair, halted, glanced at the note paper and book in his hand and laid them abruptly on his desk. He turned to face Costa, but he did not sit down. "One of the real cattlemen of the old West, Earle, or you might say one of the cattlemen of the real old West. One of the men who helped to make the West. He's owned the Iron Kettle for thirty years. He had owned it for five years when I first became acquainted with him."

"How did you ever run into him?" Costa interrupted.

"How did I make my money?" Taight countered dryly, and suddenly resumed his pacing, unable to remain calmly motionless. "In the cattle business. In the old days I was making trips west and buying cattle from different ranches, shipping the cattle east to the yards. It was on one of those trips that I ran across Lew Sudler at the Iron Kettle. He had a fine bunch of stock. I knew I was lucky to get them.

"Ever since, I have been buying every head of beef he'd sell. But it isn't business only that has kept alive the bond between Lew and me. We just hit it off. I don't see him usually more than once or twice a year. Long after I quit active buying and retired from my real participation in the detailed business of the syndicate, I always went to ship Lew's cattle. I still go at intervals, to laze around in Montana at the Iron Kettle, to shoot elk and deer, and pop off a few coyotes on the side for fun. But mostly to talk to Lew."

"Very interesting," Costa put in. "But it doesn't tell me what kind of man he is—to any extent."

"Well," Taight paused in his pacing to smile at the detective. "He packs a gun that would blow a hole through you big enough to ram your finger in. He rides a horse nobody else can ride, a big rawboned ugly tempered brute of his own choosing. He lives like any of his cowpunchers. Is one of them. Rides with them, eats with them, works with them and fights with them—I mean shoulder to shoulder.

"You'd never know he owned the ranch, if you waited to find it out from him. He'd chase a cattle thief to Jericho, battle at the least excuse and be the last one to quit. He'd walk ten miles to pay a dollar when it's due, and he hates walking like the devil. Can't even go shut a gate without riding his horse to the job. He'd give you the shirt off his back when he was freezing, if you needed it. He'd hand you his last flapjack when he was starving, if you were hungry, and say he'd just had a full meal. *But*—he wouldn't ask for a lift of any kind unless—well, I simply can't figure Lew asking for help."

"Ah!" The detective's brows raised slightly. "Your friend Lew Sudler is the epitome of independence, I infer. Then, when he says S.O.S. it means—"

"S.O.S.!" Taight returned vehemently.

"Which is exactly what I wanted to know. I should advise you to reach Montana with all possible speed. But your private car is out of the question. What's the most powerful automobile you have?"

"The green touring. I've done ninety with it."

"Then it's the green touring, and off for Montana tonight." An ironic twinkle lit the hazel eyes. "I suppose it *will* hold two?"

"Two!" Taight halted in his restless pacing to shoot an amazed glance at the detective. "It'll hold seven. Why? *You're* not going!"

"What's to stop me?" Costa smiled, stretched in his chair and eyed his pipe reproachfully. It had gone out. "Your picture of Sudler is very clear. Viewing it from all angles, a number of things are very clear." He paused, frowning a little, and Taight, knowing him, asked rather sharply;

"Just what have you figured out?"

"Well, he is evidently a prisoner under the observant eye of guards. A 'damned ugly outfit' would hardly mean as few as two or three persons. The book he sent you isn't a thing he'd be carrying about, but he evidently had it in what ever place they are detaining him. It seems to me a logical deduction that he must be imprisoned in his own house. He might have had a dozen hymn books. Because you never saw one there isn't definite proof that he never had any. And he is, I would say, so closely watched that he is unable to get assistance from any nearby source. So he conceives the idea of sending across the continent to you, in such a manner that this damned ugly outfit will not have the least suspicion he's sending for help. Of course, they wouldn't allow him to write a letter. But they would let him send a birthday gift to an old friend over two thousand miles away."

"Anything else?" Taight asked in mild sarcasm.

"They allowed that," Costa went on as though he had not heard, "Provided he allowed them to examine the gift, be certain it contained no communication, write the inscription themselves, wrap and mail it. Which accounts for the handwriting not being his own. He had to take a chance that they would not discover the pinholes in the hymn. I have an idea he drew the brands before he asked them to send the book, and they probably thought nothing of seeing the Iron Kettle facsimile on the flyleaf."

"The chances are they're a bunch of dumb bells," Taight said irritably. "And wouldn't know how to decipher those pin pricks if they found them."

"You don't really believe that, do you?" Costa laughed, and Taight looked him in the eye in surprise. Costa went on amusedly. "With all respect to your friend Sudler, Bruce, that's about the most elementary kind of secret message he could have sent you. It's puerile and melodramatic. But he had to do the best he could under the circumstances. He's in a tight pinch and knows his life isn't worth the snap of a finger unless help comes with short delay. He'll be pushing up the daisies, or the cacti, or whatever grows out there, if you don't answer that call as quickly as steam and gas can take you."

"Hell, man!" Taight cut in, his eyes widening in consternation. "Do you think it's that bad?"

"I shouldn't think you'd need me to tell you that." Costa knocked the dottle from his pipe and began packing it afresh. "But going out there in your private car would be a grave mistake. It would call down too much attention. Those fellows have certainly threatened him with instant death if he made any attempt to reach anybody. That Latin phrase he used had more purpose than merely carrying a desperate appeal to you. It sounds odd enough to stick in the minds of the men who mailed the package. And they'll remember that it was sent to New York. It's an obvious play to mislead them. And it's obvious, also, that you're his sole chance for aid, the only person he could turn to for help, the only man he can possibly reach. 'At the point of death—My Faith Looks Up To Thee.' Humph! And you ask if it's that bad."

"But how are we going to get there in time?" Taight demanded, appalled. "Why should anyone place Lew Sudler in such a desperate position as that? What could he have done to call down on himself such vindictive persecution?"

"That's what we've got to find out," Costa returned. "We'll pull up at the Iron Kettle in about four days and—"

"Four days! You're crazy!" Taight ejaculated. "By automobile? It'll take two weeks!"

"Oh, we'll ship the touring, man. Ship it, and get off at the nearest town. How far is it from Miles City?"

"Well, the roads are pretty rough, but we could reach the Iron Kettle in a day's travel from Miles City, if we drive like the devil."

"And you can," Costa grinned. "We'll get off at

Miles City then. You, come to think of it, Bruce, don't look at all well. You're suffering from over worked nerves and too close confinement."

"*Me?* What the—?" Taight glared, and Costa laughed aloud.

"Yes, you. I, as your personal physician, advise you to get out into the air for a protracted period. As a matter of fact, a slow leisurely trip to the west coast would be ideal for you. And I, as your personal physician, realizing your bullheaded stubbornness and your dislike for taking orders, will be obliged to go along and see that you don't disobey any of my dictates."

"Oh!" Taight grinned in return.

"Yes, oh." Costa nodded and got to his feet.

"But see here, Earle," Taight protested. "That's old stuff."

Costa shrugged. "Everything is. But it'll work. Fellows are getting bad nerves and being ordered out from close confinement every day. And that's about as logical and workable a stall as I can think of right now. And then, I am a doctor, you know."

"Yes," the millionaire snorted in disgust. "But the punkest doctor this side of New Guinea wouldn't accuse me of having nerves. I'm strong as a bull, and look it. Nerves!"

"Oh, not your motor nerves. Your sensory nerves." Costa grinned at him again. "The evidence of those doesn't show so much, only in temper, and you've got that. The point is not what's the matter with you, but that we reach the Iron Kettle with all possible speed and have a handy alibi for being in that vicinity. So, in about four days we'll arrive at the ranch and announce ourselves as Doctor Earle Costa and his patient Mr Bruce Taight, on a trip for the patient's health. Are you as good a liar as I am?"

"Try me."

"All right. We've got to make those fellows believe that you're sick even though you don't look it, that we have been traveling leisurely for some three weeks, and have merely stopped enroute to see your old friend Sudler. Manifestly, this outfit will see that we must have left the east coast long before that package was sent from the Iron Kettle. Mr Bruce Taight from Florida doesn't sound much like Mr Articulo Mortis from New York. They'll never for a moment connect us in any way with the birthday present. I suppose you can manage to get your automobile on the flyer that leaves this evening, can't you?"

Taight glanced at the clock on the wall as he rose to accompany the detective to the door. "Four hours. I can. And secure a couple of berths besides. I'll stop for you at six fifteen sharp."

"Thanks," Costa paused at the door. "Don't tell your chauffeur or any of your staff where you're going. Tell 'em you're still in Florida."

"Why?"

"Because I say so. Who's running this show? And by the way, have you got the least idea who any of these fellows in this so-called 'damned ugly outfit' might be?"

Taight frowned. "I don't know, Earle. I've been thinking I may make a close guess at the leader of the crew. There's a pretty notorious fellow cutting a wide swath out in that part of the country right now. He's known as the Malo Hombre."

"Hmmm—. Sounds theatrical," Costa commented. "What's it mean?"

"Spanish for bad man, Earle. And I guess he lives up to it. If we can get our hands on the Malo Hombre, I've an idea it'll be all over but the shouting."

"Is that a hunch?" Costa inquired.

"A hunch?" Taight laughed shortly. "I never have 'em. But—yes. It's a hunch. Get me?"

"Yes. I think I do." Costa nodded, and favored the millionaire with a dry smile. "See you later," he nodded again and stepped out the door, leaving Bruce Taight standing by his desk, frowning to himself and absentmindedly drumming on the flat top with his fingers.

Abruptly Taight rang for Albers, and when the butler appeared at the door, the master requested crisply:

"Albers—bring me those newspaper clippings concerning the Malo Hombre."

As Albers went to accomplish his errand, Taight

still stood drumming his fingers thoughtfully on the desk top, and once, shortly, he muttered to himself: “The Malo Hombre—. Yes, it’s a hunch.”

Chapter II

CYNARA

Two hours later Bruce Taight was still sitting before his desk. He had ordered the packing of grip and bag. The green automobile had been rushed to the depot and an extra express car had been attached to the flyer. The automobile now reposed in the express car waiting the hour of departure. A stateroom and two berths were being held for Taight, until he should arrive at the station and choose between them. And Bruce Taight had not left his desk. Money. And a telephone.

With a sigh of relief Taight raised a hand to ring for the butler. The bell clamored musically somewhere in the distance. The master of the house looked up as the door opened and the butler stood before him.

“Albers,” Taight began. “Just a word. I wish you would tell the rest of the staff—” He was interrupted by the resonant clanging of the door gong, down the hall. He shifted impatiently in his chair. “Damn the doorbell! Albers, I’m not at home. Not to anyone, mind!”

Albers nodded and went to answer the bell. Taight heard him speak. A woman’s voice answered and Taight heard the front door shut. Their voices were so lowered that Taight could catch no words, but he knew the woman had entered the hall. The voices grew swiftly nearer. Then Albers threw open the door, glanced at his master deprecatingly, and said with an apologetic shrug:

"It's Miss Cynara, sir."

Instantly Taight was on his feet, surprise in his eyes and a smile on his face, had rounded the desk and hurried toward the woman.

"Cynara!" His smile was superseded by a startled expression as he noted her white face and shadowed eyes. He took her hands in both of his. "I thought I left you safe and sound in Florida a few weeks ago!"

"Yes, you did, Dad." Her fingers gripped back. "But I followed you. I got tired of the pace."

Taight frowned, then nodded briskly. "Of course. You couldn't do anything but come home. You just relax and rest. I won't be home for a few weeks. No one knows I've come back from that last trip yet. And I don't want them to know. I want everyone to think I am still in Florida."

"But Dad!" Cynara's face blanched and she leaned toward him in panic. "I thought your business trip was done. Where are you going? It isn't imperative, is it? Put it off, for a while, anyway."

"I'm sorry, Cynara, but that's impossible."

"Why? Oh, that's miserable! For you to have something calling you away right at this time. You can't go, Dad! I'm tired out, so tired I'm half sick. Does anyone need you worse than I do?"

"I don't know, Cynara. But I rather suspect so. You've heard me speak of Lew Sudler, my rancher friend out in Montana. He has sent for me. He is in desperate straits of some kind. With you, it means only a few weeks of loneliness at worst, and then I'll be back. But if I refuse to go to Lew, it may mean his life. Earle Costa is going with me."

"Costa, the detective?"

"Yes. When I got in last night that thing there was waiting for me. The message from Lew is concealed in the book. Look." Taight picked up the book and paper lying on his desk and carried them around to her. He opened the book to the marked hymn, showed her the pinholes Costa had blackened and the decoded message written on the paper. "So you see, my dear, I must go. There's no way out of it. When Lew sends a call as mysterious and sinister as that it means something pretty bad."

"Then take me, too," Cynara demanded. "Costa won't care. I know Earle. Take me with you."

"I can't do that either, Cynara." Taight shook his head. "There's an ugly mixup of some kind out there. It's no place for a woman. There isn't a woman on the ranch. Lew's a bachelor, though he isn't old. He can work and fight and ride as hard as any of his punchers and there isn't a grey hair on his head. That's why I know he's desperate. Lew Sudler—sending out an S.O.S. and saying he's at the point of death! Cynara! Can you really ask me not to go?"

"No, I guess not." Cynara shook her head. "I won't ask that any more. I just ask you to take me, too. I'm not afraid. The more danger and excitement there is the better I'll like it. So long as you're there. My grips are all packed too, and they're also at the station in the baggage room. I was going to send the chauffeur for them tomorrow. Couldn't you get me a ticket and a berth?"

"Oh yes, I could do it. It's easy enough to get the tickets, and I've already got two berths and a stateroom held for me. Earle and I could take the berths and you could have the stateroom, I suppose. But, no! I won't do it, Cynara. It's impossible."

"It isn't." Cynara was on her feet again, both hands catching at his arm, as she went on swiftly: "You haven't anything to say about it, Dad. I'm going, and if you won't buy me a ticket and a berth, I'll pay my way on the train and sit up in the observation car at night. They can't put me off as long as I pay my way. I'm going, I tell you!"

Taight eyed her for a moment in perplexed

silence. Then he grinned ruefully to himself. Verily, he had no choice in the matter. He shrugged and walked back to his desk.

"All right," he said shortly. "You're a headstrong little fool, Cynara, just as you always were. But I guess it's the only way out, and I'll have to stand for it. You may go. Sit down, now, and let me phone in for another ticket. And call Earle. He may raise the devil, but there's no help for it. You women! You can get a man into a jam quicker than anything else on earth. And then some damned fools ask Lew why he never married!"

Cynara smiled. "That's right, go on and cuss. You sound natural when you cuss."

Taight ignored her, frowning into the telephone as he called the ticket office, then hung up to disconnect and call Costa.

"Hello, Earle?" Taight spoke tersely. "Say, I've got to take a woman along. Yeh, that's what I said, a woman. Oh, damn it anyhow, I don't know. I can't explain. She's sitting right here grinning at me. Huh? Do you know her? Sure! It's Cynara. Huh? What? Oh, that's all right then? The hell it is! Yeh, we'll be there in thirty minutes to pick you up." And he hung up the receiver with a bang.

"I suppose you're satisfied now?" He glared at Cynara. "You've got your way."

"Oh, don't growl at me," Cynara retorted

calmly. "Tell me about this place where we're going. How big is it? It must be a huge place. Maybe two hundred acres? And a thousand cattle or so?"

Taight laughed aloud. "Is that your idea of a huge place? That's what Lew would call a truck garden. He has something over twelve thousand acres and upwards of eight thousand head of cattle. The territory is wild. The hills are peppered with three or four kinds of bad men, rustlers, bandits and sheriffs. Not to speak of swearing, drinking, fighting punchers who work the ranches. Want to back out?"

"No, not me. You can't scare me with such childish bugaboos."

"They aren't bugaboos," Taight returned soberly. "I mean exactly what I say. And I'm referring to real bad men, the kind they have in the West. The kind that tote a pair of guns big enough for young cannons, ride a brute of a horse, drink a barrel of whiskey for breakfast and shoot the eyebrows off coyotes for target practice in the evening."

"Now I know you're spoofing," Cynara smiled. "The only kind of man I have any use for anyway is the kind that is just a man, and you're the only one I know."

"Now who's spoofing?" Taight grinned broadly. "Be that as it may, put on your hat and let's be moving. Earle's waiting for us." He shoved the hymn book and piece of notepaper into his desk, locked the drawer, shoved the key in his pocket and reached to jab the bell button. Albers appeared promptly at the door.

"Albers—" Taight glanced at him as he spoke. "I'll tell you now what I was going to tell you when I called you in a while ago. I am rushing away on a hurried business trip of great importance. Where I'm going doesn't matter. You won't be able to reach me. Miss Cynara will accompany me. No one is to know I got back here at all. Instruct the rest of the staff. To any inquiry concerning me, simply say that I have not yet returned from Florida. That's all."

"Yes sir. Very well, sir." Albers made a mental note of his duty and went on about his business.

Exactly thirty minutes later Taight's sedan stopped before the apartment house in which Earle Costa resided. The detective came down the stairs briskly, shoved his grip into the tonneau and took a seat by Cynara.

Two hours more, and the flyer was racing out of the city limits, picking up speed as its wheels hummed over the rails. In the seventh car Bruce Taight, Earle Costa and Cynara Taight speculated on what manner of sinister predicament must obtain at the Iron Kettle.

Chapter III
ENIGMA

Here one goes back twenty years, to the Iron Kettle.

Lew Sudler had then owned the ranch for ten years. He had not at one time come into possession of the whole twelve thousand acres finally comprising the Iron Kettle. The ranch had encompassed but twelve hundred acres when he first purchased it. Sudler loved the land. He loved space. From time to time, through the ten years succeeding his settling there he bought other lands adjacent and added to his holdings, until he acquired the twelve thousand acres and the Iron Kettle had grown to be one of the largest ranches in the West.

To the west of him, his line ended where the Floating R began. The Floating R was in comparison a new ranch, the property of Kurt Ridelle. The nearest ranch to the north was the Cross Eight, a very new ranch which was not doing well. The Cross Eight and the Floating R, with miles intervening, were Lew Sudler's closest neighbors, and would remain so, because he owned the land between. To the east and south, only uninhabited plains and hills rolled away from the Iron Kettle.

Along the south line of the ranch lay a small strip of five hundred acres, the last piece of land Sudler had purchased. At one corner of the five hundred there squatted a forlorn old cabin upon a small cleared space. A taciturn little Dutchman had at one time some years before taken up a homestead there and built the cabin. He suddenly deserted his homestead, and departed as unobtrusively as he had come. Nothing was ever heard of him again. But the old cabin still remained.

When Sudler purchased that five hundred acres, he bought from the government the homestead relinquishment the Dutchman had left behind. Having no particular reason for razing the cabin, the rancher allowed it to stand. Some thirty miles beyond it in the same direction lay the little town of Dry Rock, where Sudler and a half a dozen other ranchers procured their provisions. The stage road running to Dry Rock, in its various windings passed three or four times within sight of Lew Sudler's south line, and of the Dutchman's old cabin.

On a hot summer afternoon one of Sudler's punchers, returning from Dry Rock, as he passed a turn in the road, chanced to glance idly across at the old cabin. And he pulled his horse to a sudden halt. A thin wisp of smoke was rising from the old mud chimney.

The cabin was a scant five miles from the Iron

Kettle ranch buildings. The puncher arrived at the ranch house something over an hour later, and reported to Sudler that the Dutchman's old cabin was occupied.

"I didn't see nothing of a man around," the puncher explained. "All I seen was a woman and a kid. But they sure must be intending to stay a while, and they ain't poverty stricken, if I'm any judge. Her and the kid was both dressed good, and I took a look into that old roothouse right next to the cabin as I came away. She's got it plumb full of provisions. Enough canned goods, flour, beans, bacon and such truck to last her a year. I didn't want to ask too many questions, and she sure didn't hand out no information. Just thought I'd tell you."

The next day Lew Sudler rode up to the Dutchman's cabin. The woman received him with a strange apathy under which there lurked a hostile alertness, a ready antagonism against anyone who sought to concern himself with her affairs. Although she was in her early twenties, her hair was quite grey. She was crippled rather horribly, and the very sight of her misshapen body under her delicate gentle face gripped Sudler sharply and moved him to a pity he seldom felt.

He remarked that one of his punchers had noted from the stage road evidences that the ancient cabin was now occupied. He added that he had ridden over to offer his services should there be anything he could do to make her more comfortable. She received the information and acknowledged his friendly intentions with a kind of grudging graciousness. She told him as much as she deemed wise to tell, and no more.

She had come west seeking a place of retirement. At Dry Rock they had told her of this deserted homestead, and she had immediately decided that it was well suited to her desire for seclusion. Her name was Mrs Leddby. She had brought with her a five-year-old son, Jay. She told Jay to speak nicely to the gentleman, and Jay eyed Sudler with the wide, curious gaze of a child.

That was all Sudler ever learned of her. He never told her she was living on his land. He went out of his way to do for her what he could. Fresh game and fresh beef frequently found their way to the cabin. The punchers, coming to and from the town, saw to it that any failing supplies were replenished. They saw to it also that there were bags of candy often brought to the child. They would have been glad to have offered to Mrs Leddby also the candy and rare treats of fruit that reached Dry Rock.

But her chill reserve abashed them, and they satisfied themselves by bringing Jay candy and fruit for both. Little Jay had enough candy to feed a horse. Once in a while Lew would remark casually that Mrs Leddby's wood was running low. The next day a handful of punchers would appear within the vicinity of the cabin, and soon neatly split wood would be stacked up all over the place.

So Mrs Leddby fared well. She accepted Sudler's kindness with that grudging graciousness which never failed, and which grew wistful toward the end. But she never talked any more than was required of her by courtesy, and all she ever told of herself amounted to precisely nothing. For four years she and the child lived on that place in isolated loneliness. For four years little Jay had for companions Lew and the punchers, and his mother. He was not conscious of the isolation.

Only vague memories lived afterward in his mind of that strange boyhood on a lost homestead in the hills of Montana. Even to Jay, his mother was "queer"—damning word! She spoke so little. And the little she did say seemed so strange. Yet, fragments of those things that she had said afterward attained sharp significance. She had impressed upon him powerfully her intense hatred for good men.

"It's a crooked world, Jay," he remembered she had said. "A beastly crooked world. Good men! I have nothing for these good men but contempt. Some of the bad men are the best. Remember that."

Jay's mind was too undeveloped to comprehend the fact that her brain was nearly as badly warped as her body. It was not possible for him to divine how sadly her heart was dragged. He only knew that through that constantly repeated belief of hers he came to have a deep admiration for bad men. He asked her once if Lew Sudler was a bad man. She said: "He carries a gun. I fancy he knows how to use it. He swears royally, even before you. I guess he isn't too good."

Jay immediately felt that he liked Lew Sudler all the better. He had liked his father. But all he could remember of that vanished man was a curling mop of flaming red hair, and a pair of twinkling eyes above a beard and mustache that matched the ruddy hair. He wished his father hadn't gone away. He felt that they two could have had a great time out here. But Mother said that Father had been gone for a long time now, and wasn't coming back. So, if he wasn't coming back, Jay had an idea that he should like to have somebody in his place. And of all the fellows on the Iron Kettle, he liked Lew best.

As for Sudler, he had begun to feel a deep personal interest in the child. An odd silent boy, Jay was. Heavy red-brown hair climbed back in deep waves from his broad high brow. What Lew noticed most about him was the strange profound glow that existed eternally in his red-brown eyes. It radiated from the pupil through the iris, coming from unguessed fathoms within. The boy seldom smiled or laughed aloud, but the glow was always there.

Lew Sudler told himself he would never forget that extraordinary glow in Jay's eyes. He told himself, regardless of where or when, in defiance of any veil the years could raise between, he would know that glow again anywhere this side of hell. He returned the boy's affection with interest. Compound interest.

Jay passed his ninth birthday. Sudler took him over to the Iron Kettle to see the marvelous birthday cake the Chinese cook had baked. Jay was very much enamoured of the cake, but he insisted that it was to be shared among his friends the punchers. He had another one at home which his mother had made. He compromised on taking a small slice to her from this one the Iron Kettle cook had made. The cowboys gave him a gala day, and in the afternoon one of them started home with him. His pockets were filled with various gifts from the boys. A mouth organ, a handful of marbles, and sundry other things dear to the heart of a boy.

But the gift from Lew was to Jay the ninth wonder of the world. It consisted of a pair of black angora chaps, made especially to fit the boy by the saddle maker in Dry Rock, a saddle and bridle made by the same man, the saddle fashioned perfectly to Jay's small body. The wonder of wonders was a rangy sturdy little pony to go with saddle and bridle. Arrayed in his finery, the boy rode his pony home, alongside the puncher who grinned at him sociably and turned back with a wave of the hand when they had come within sight of the cabin.

Jay was desirous of making a very dramatic entrance. He even considered for a moment the attractive idea of riding the pony right into the cabin, but thought better of it. He compromised by riding at a soft walk, so Mrs Leddby wouldn't hear, to within ten feet of the cabin door. There he dismounted, gave his chaps a hitch, cocked his hat on one side of his head, hauled out the mouth organ and marched into the cabin blowing upon it with all his might. The sound he achieved was merely a blatant announcement of his arrival, but it was a soul satisfying cacophony to his young ears. (He had, after all, forgotten the slice of cake for his mother.) Thrilled to the toes with all the marvelous things he had to show and tell, he came to the middle of the cabin floor.

And there he halted. His mother lay on her bed, in a twisted heap that chilled his heart and turned the glow in his eyes to the black glare of terror. He tried to call to her, but his voice stuck in his throat. He whirled and raced out of the cabin, and his terror sent his voice into a shrill scream after Sudler's puncher. But the cowboy was already out of sight and hearing. The boy whirled again, raced back into the cabin, stumbled to a stop and went with faltering feet toward the bed. Then he was suddenly on his knees, frantically gripping his mother's arm, calling her in a panic stricken cry.

"Mother! I am here! I'm here, Mother!"

Mrs Leddby stirred and opened her eyes, staring at him vaguely, as though she were puzzled at his presence and was striving to find some reason for his being there. She was so far beyond the touch of corporeal things that even her voice was strange to him.

"You? Yes—who?"

"It's me!" The boy's terror rose. Something was here that he did not understand. He had never heard of death. He did not know there was such a word, nor such a transition. He cried again; "It's me—Jay."

The name seemed to awaken some memory in her wandering thoughts. She smiled. Jay always remembered that she was very beautiful when she smiled. And he always remembered what she said then.

"Jay. J stands for Jason. Jason Aaron Orme. That is a beautiful name. Jason Aaron Orme. You must go to Jason—in Louisiana."

She did not speak again. Her eyes fixed on the ceiling, and the smile fixed on her face. But she spoke no more. She did not move any more, and the boy's terror overcame him. He shrank from her. From that awe-striking smile. He stumbled away from the bed and ran out of the house. He knew of but one place to go, to the Iron Kettle, to Lew Sudler. It was five miles, but he did not know that. It would have made no difference if he had known it. He had to go somewhere, to get someone.

He climbed on to his little pony, turned its head toward the Iron Kettle, and lashed it into a run. When he reached the ranch house in little over a half hour's time, the pony's hide was wet with sweat and the animal was blowing and heaving from its exertion. Sudler came dashing out of the house, leaped the lane fence, snatched the boy into his arms and demanded to know what was wrong. But even before the boy spoke, he knew.

"Mother!" Jay gasped. "She's funny. She won't talk. She won't move. She just looks at the ceiling and smiles. I'm afraid."

Sudler had been expecting it. He had seen that she was failing. He hitched his team to the buckboard and drove at high speed to the homestead. Nothing was in the bare cabin to tell him anything more than he now knew. He went back to the Iron Kettle with the woman's body wrapped in blankets lying in the bed of the wagon, and with the boy sobbing himself to sleep on the seat at his side.

Soberly and respectfully the rancher and his punchers carried her to the top of a long slope overlooking the ranch from the north. They knew no prayers, and felt too solemn to sing. They buried her in silence, and buried with her all she had refused to tell. They laid her under three great pine trees with her face toward the west. Over her head they rolled a massive rock, and on it Lew Sudler chiseled six words.

MRS LEDDBY DIED AND AT REST

Chapter IV

JASON—IN LOUISIANA

Sudler tried to explain to the bewildered boy. His explanation of the transition was a thing of solemn dignity, had he known it, but only a few scattered phrases lodged in Jay's mind. Ever after, the boy thought of death as something that made people say queer things, and smile, and stop moving.

It ensued as a matter of course that the boy should stay on at the Iron Kettle. After a while Sudler and some of his men emptied the cabin and tore it down. He found nothing anywhere which could give him the slightest information concerning the woman who had died there. He wondered anew from what harsh circumstance she had fled; what maiming cataclysm had numbered the days of the woman who lay at the top of the slope under the pine trees and the big stone.

Lew went back to the ranch after the remains of the cabin were burned, feeling anxiously duty bound to find the boy's relatives if possible. Troubled, he asked Jay if he had any idea where he might reach his father.

"Can't you remember what his name was, Jay?

What did he look like? He didn't die, too, did he?"

Soberly the boy shook his head, and the glow in the red-brown eyes stilled. "No, I can't remember what his name was. I can't remember how he looked, only he had curly red hair and a red beard. But he didn't say any queer things. He didn't say anything at all. And he didn't smile. He scowled, something awful. And he could move. So I guess he wasn't dead. They said he just went away." The earnest eyes were fastened regretfully on Lew's face.

The past had become a closed book to Jay, and the great stone bearing the terse epitaph weighed down effectually the lids of the book. So Lew considered it a settled issue and accepted the boy gratefully as a gift from life.

He set himself to entertain the child and make him forget his grief. He made him a present of an old Colt .44 that would fire no more. The boy had coaxed persistently for a gun. After Sudler gave it to him, he asked the rancher if he would be a bad man if he carried a gun and learned to swear. Sudler stared at him curiously, said no, not necessarily, and asked why.

"Because I want to be a bad man," Jay informed him gravely, the glow in his eyes warm and alive with eagerness. "My mother, she didn't like good men. Good men are bad, and bad men are good. That's what she said. So I want to be a bad man."

Lew had nothing to say to that. All through summer and fall Jay rode his pony around the ranch and carried the harmless old gun as though it were a treasure. But he was not content.

A strange restlessness had seized him. He did not tell Sudler. He felt that he must go away to Louisiana—to find that Jason man. But he didn't want to hurt Lew's feelings. He didn't want Lew to think that he was ungrateful for his kindness. He loved Lew and he loved the Iron Kettle. And even though he went away, he knew he would come back. So he kept it to himself.

And he took it out in going farther from the ranch buildings every time he went for a ride. One of the men at the south line camp had his small son with him, and Jay formed a habit of riding over to see the other boy. Now and then he asked Lew's permission to stay at the line camp overnight. Sudler, sensing the child's yearning for companionship of his own age, good-naturedly gave his consent. Two or three times Jay went and stayed of his own accord, without asking permission.

Then the winter came and he was confined much of the time to the house. During the long evenings and bitterly cold days he had endless hours for brooding. He was not inherently moody, but the events of his life had served to cast a somber shadow upon him. Day after day he would sit and brood as he stared, trance-like, at the glowing red sides of the iron stove. For a while no coherent sequence of ideas took shape in his musing. The child thought of many things: of how queer death was, of the deer he had seen on the hills, of how fast his pony could run, of how much he liked Lew, of how strange it was that Lew should want to know about his father.

Out of the scattered thoughts, his mind began to pivot upon that certain thing—Lew's asking about his father. It was gradually borne in upon him that so far as he knew his father was alive somewhere. And if he were alive, Jay decided he ought to find him as well as that Jason, though he hadn't the least idea of how to go about it. When the snow was gone and the fields were green again, he would go and find the man with twinkling eyes and red hair and Jason Aaron Orme, and they would all come back to the Iron Kettle and live with Lew.

It is only a step from imaginative brooding to the conception of a profound determination.

It was nearing spring, then, and the thaw was already under way. Jay waited impatiently for the melting snow to be gone.

And one day the last snow faded, the sun shone.

The next day he took his pony and went for a ride. That night he did not come home. Sudler grinned to himself and guessed that Jay had gone to the line camp to spend the night with the puncher's boy. He did not become really uneasy for three days. Then, when the boy had not returned, the rancher rode over to the line camp looking for him. But Jay was not there, and had not been there. Startled, shaken with swift alarm, Sudler whirled his horse and galloped home.

In the overwhelming sense of loss that swept down upon him, the rancher realized how much the boy had grown into his life. For a week everything on the Iron Kettle stopped. Every puncher on the ranch rode the hills and plains in an ever-widening circle. But nowhere was there any trace of the boy. They did not come upon a mangled body that could testify mutely how wild animals had slain him. They did not find his pony anywhere. No one had seen Jay or knew anything of him. Baffled and grieved, Sudler and his men were finally forced to admit defeat. Both boy and pony had disappeared as completely as a shadow dissipated in the sun, or a light blown out in the dark.

The old routine began again on the ranch, with the sole difference that little Jay was gone. But the child's personality had made a powerful impression on the heart and mind of Lew Sudler. Although Jay had vanished, hope lingered persistently in Sudler's brain. Somewhere, sometime, perhaps years hence, Jay would hear the call of his heart and come back to the Iron Kettle. It might be a very long time. The child might have grown to a man before that should come to pass.

But Jay would return. And Sudler knew that he would recognize him.

"I sure will," the rancher muttered to himself, raising his gaze to the three pine trees at the top of the slope. "I'll know that shine in his eyes if he's a hundred years old. I'll know it anywhere this side of hell."

Chapter V

JAY IN SEARCH OF HIS FATHER

Jay was many miles from the Iron Kettle; he did not know how many. He was hungry and his lunch was gone, but he couldn't turn back. He had come in sight of a strange ranch house and saw a light in the window. He decided he would stop there and ask for his supper. But what would he tell the people in the house? If he told them his name they would send him back to the Iron Kettle. Lew would be looking for him, might even send the men out after him.

Then quite suddenly Jay knew what he would tell the people in the ranch house. He would say he was going to his father. But he would pretend craftily that he had just a little way further to go, though he had failed to reach his destination before night fell. He would ask for something to eat and a place to sleep. But they would be sure to ask his name, and he must have a name to tell them. Abruptly he remembered what his mother had said. "J stands for Jason. Jason Aaron Orme. That is a beautiful name." Jay decided that it did sound rather well. He would adopt it. He would say he was Jason Aaron Orme, going to his father. Then they wouldn't send him back to the Iron Kettle.

He found in the ranch house an old cattleman and his wife. He told them exactly what he had planned to tell. He told it very honestly. They took his story at face value and thought nothing of it. And in that strange ranch house he slept. The next morning the rancher's wife gave him a lunch, and he started on again. That night was a repetition of the one before. As was the next, and then next. Three days later the boy was nearly a hundred miles away from the Iron Kettle. He had decided now that he would go to Louisiana and find that Jason man first. Maybe Jason Orme knew where his father was. Maybe that was the quickest way to find his father. So he began asking the way to Louisiana.

The days became weeks, and the weeks became months. Jay never remembered those next five months very clearly. They lived but dimly in his mind afterward, dream-like, as a long panorama of hazy travel, of stops at ranch houses, villages and towns. He avoided cities instinctively. Down hills and through forests, across valleys and skirting mountains he progressed steadily. The pony cropped grass, drank from mountain streams and valley springs, accepted occasional bread crusts with gratitude, and grew thin. He had been fat as a butter ball when that incredible journey began. He was lean and gaunt when it ended, near the outskirts of a little town in Louisiana.

Pony and boy approached the town as it was growing dusk. They went along a quiet road shaded by green trees such as Jay had never seen before, and cotton fields stretched away on either hand. They came opposite the entrance way to an old Southern estate, and the boy drew his pony to a halt with a gasp of astonishment. He saw something he had never seen before—fireflies, dozens of them, sailing over the China trees and water oaks like living intermittent sparks. One seemed brighter than the rest. It swooped in front of him and lighted on a gate post at the entrance of the driveway leading into the estate. Jay got off his horse and walked toward it. It did not flit away as he approached, but remained motionless on the gate post, winking and glowing and luring him.

As he reached out a hand to touch it, he glanced beyond into the confines of the estate. Inside the gateway great trees shaded rolling lawns before the shadowy bulk of an antique pillared house. A man standing on the lawn, an indistinct figure in the dusk, glanced curiously at the boy. Jay gave him no attention. He was interested solely in the firefly. It stayed very still and he took it in his hand. The man strolled toward him, halted within a few feet of him and stood eyeing boy and pony. It was quite evident to him that they had come a long way.

“Good evening, son,” the man greeted him. “Where are you going?”

“I’m going to see my father,” Jay answered glibly, with the facility of long practice. “It’s just a little way farther, but I couldn’t make it before night.”

“You’d better come into my house and get something to eat for yourself and your horse,” the man suggested. “You both look as though a little food wouldn’t hurt you. How far have you come?”

“From Montana,” Jay answered absent-mindedly, staring at the firefly. It suddenly flew out of his hand and he raised his face to watch it as it sailed into the air.

The man uttered an exclamation of sharp surprise. As the boy turned up his face, he saw the red-brown eyes glowing in the small thin face. He stared into them for a long time.

“Come in,” he said abruptly, and gestured toward the walk leading to the big house. Without question or hesitation Jay nodded acquiescence and started up the walk. The man stepped to the pony, caught its reins in one hand and followed the boy.

At a corner of the house he called to an old negro a little way beyond and told him to take the pony to the rambling stable that bulked like a great blot of shadow in a grove of water oaks in the rear of the house. Then he led the boy up the steps to the pillared porch. In the house he set out a lunch and sat down across the table from the boy. For a long while he studied Jay's face in silence. Finally, with an odd reluctance, like a man who is afraid of what he may hear, he said, "You haven't told me your name."

"Oh." Jay looked up. "My name is Jason Aaron Orme." The man stiffened in his chair. He cried out as though something had stung him, and his face whitened. Jay stared. "What's the matter?" the boy demanded. "What's the matter with that name?"

"Nothing." The man spoke as though something choked him. "Nothing. Only—it happens to be my name, too."

Jay stopped eating. "Well," he said at last, after a long quiet pause, "I *came* to find my father. They just call me Jay."

"But I am not your father," Orme answered, and his eyes were bleak. "I am not your father, Jay, but I know where he is. I am your father's brother." Orme halted, scrutinizing the boy closely. "Where is—*she?*"

"You mean my mother?" Jay asked. His mother was the only woman he had ever known. Orme nodded, and Jay explained. "Oh, she's back there in Montana. Something happened to her. Lew said it was death. She wouldn't move and she wouldn't talk. She wouldn't do nothing but smile. I didn't like the way she smiled. Lew didn't either. He put her in the ground and rolled a big stone over her. I didn't like that. But Lew said you always do that to people when they die. I don't want to die."

"Who's Lew?" Orme cut in, as though the boy's words were unbearable and he must change their trend.

"Lew Sudler," Jay answered. "He said I could live with him. As soon as I get my father, we're going back. But I have to find him first. I got to thinking about it. Then, Mother said I had to come to you." And in short terse sentences the boy explained the thing that had happened.

So Jay came to the old house in which Ormes of many generations had been born, had lived and died. For a day or two he was interested in the plantation, the fields, the negroes and the many things in the great house. Then he became urgent about going to his father. Orme told him gently that he could not now go to his father. He must wait a little while.

"But I've got to get back to the Iron Kettle," Jay persisted. "Lew will be worrying about me."

"Yes? Well, he will have to wait, too," Orme answered.

The waiting grew. Every time Jay spoke of his father, Orme answered invariably with the one word, "Wait." Gradually the boy's insistence subsided. The Orme plantation became home. The day after he came Jason introduced him to the old negro cook, Mammy Cindy. "Cindy,"

Orme had said, "this is Jay, Master Gem's boy. Somebody else for you to baby." Jay liked Mammy Cindy immensely, but even as he looked up into her black face, he was thinking that he remembered now that that was what his mother had called his father—Gem.

He roamed around the fields, watched the negroes picking the curious fluffs of cotton, and found a measure of content. Pony and boy grew round and fat again. And though the waiting lengthened, though weeks and months wore into years, Jay never forgot that he had come to find his father, and that he was going back to the Iron Kettle and Lew.

Orme told him it was time his education began. Jay was not sensible of what an unusual and highly finished education it was. At the hands of an efficient tutor Jay learned to read and write and cipher. He was an adept scholar. Orme's wide acres stretched away in level fields beyond the great house. On these wide acres, under the training of other experts, Jay learned things that are not taught to all boys. He learned to ride and handle horses like a veteran, to break all the colts that were born on or brought to the Orme plantation. He learned to shoot with a facility and accuracy that can come only with those things practiced from early childhood.

But from no source did he learn anything concerning his father.

Chapter VI

THE END OF A WAIT

When Jay was eighteen, he could ride anything wrapped in horsehide and standing on four feet. He could break the meanest broncho that ever tried to throw a rider. He could draw and fire a six-shooter, two of them, with the speed and accuracy of the kind so phenomenal that they are to be believed only when they are seen. The day after his eighteenth birthday Orme called him into his study and silently stood contemplating him from head to foot.

Grown, Jay was not overly tall, a bare inch under six feet. Constant riding and outdoor exercise had hardened his muscles and moulded his bones. In physical appearance he had changed little. The red-brown hair climbing away from the broad high forehead was not perceptibly darkened. The strange glow, that had so lodged in the mind of Lew Sudler, was still alive in the red-brown eyes. He was broad of shoulder, thick of chest, strong of arm.

Orme nodded as he looked at him, satisfied, and began speaking.

"Jay, I am compelled to do something I dislike. I must send you back to Montana. Long ago you learned to cease asking about your father. I may tell you now that when you are twenty-five years old, you shall see him. In the interim, there are things for you to learn. I hardly know how to say this to you. But—your name was never Leddby. Neither is it Orme. Your father is only my half-brother, his surname is not the same as mine. We were never sensible of a half tie. We were as close as full-blood brothers. We spent our early youth here together, until he went west, fired by the idea of finding a gold mine in California.

"He never found it. He drifted northward to Montana, where he lived and worked for several years as a cowboy. It was there he met and married your mother. They both came south with you when you were not yet a year old. They had come only for a visit. But our mother and my father had died, and I implored them to stay with me. So we four lived on here together, for a very little while. Then, something terrible happened. All our lives were shattered. Your father disappeared, and your mother went away, taking you with her. I may tell you this now. More I cannot tell you.

"I cannot even tell you your name. I might suggest that you make a name for yourself. I have built as best I could on the solid foundation of character you inherited from your parents. When you see your father seven years hence, all the rest will be explained. There is an old agreement between him and me which must be fulfilled to the letter. Perhaps, when you know everything, you will think the conditions of that agreement wild and strange. They may be. But such as it is, the agreement stands. He has to keep his part. I must keep mine. Maybe I am warped. I think perhaps all our lives are warped—as she was warped. Do you remember?"

Jay's only answer was a somber nod. Orme went on.

"This is what I have to do: I have to send you out alone. And you must go back to Montana, to the cattle country where you were born. Do you remember ever having heard this Lew Sudler speak of the Whiskey Flask ranch?"

Jay shook his head. "No, I don't. But if I am to go back to Montana, I shall head for the Iron Kettle. You know I am determined to return to Lew."

Orme smiled, a wry grimace. "You may do that. There is no objection. But that is far in the future. Here—I have something for you." He stepped to a chair over which was thrown a great woolen shawl. He lifted the shawl and laid it on a nearby divan.

Jay's eyes riveted upon the chair and the objects so revealed. Across the back of the chair lay a faded blue flannel shirt, until now hidden by the folds of the shawl. On the chair seat lay a pair of black angora batwing chaps. Tilted against them was a black Stetson hat with a high crown and broad brim. Upon the shirt reposed a faded crimson and blue bandana neckerchief. On the brim of the hat lay a pair of spurs to fit the high heeled boots next to them. The whole outfit had the air of things well cherished and preserved. The faded shirt was spotlessly clean. The leather in boots and chaps had been kept pliable. The long angora hair was combed free of snarls. The spurs were bright and shining.

"The outfit your father had when he came south," Orme said. "I've been keeping them for you. I knew you would come back. There was an agreement between your mother and me too. I knew she was going away after your father left. But she left without warning, one day while I was absent from home. She wrote me from Tennessee, saying that though she would never come back, she would send you after a while, so that I might keep the agreement I had made with your father.

"I tried to find her. I searched all over the States, but my search availed me nothing. She had found seclusion, and she kept her silence. I might have known she'd go back to Montana, the state where she was born. Yet, I searched Montana, too. If only she hadn't taken the name of Leddby. Where on earth did she get it? How did she ever come upon so dull and uninteresting a name. I realize now exactly what happened. She repeatedly put off sending you to me, dreading to part with you, until it was too late. Yet, dying, she remembered—and told you to come."

Jay nodded. Orme went on with abrupt briskness:

"I think that is all I have to tell you. It is your father's desire that when you have passed the age of eighteen you shall go into the life he loved, the life he considered the only one worthwhile. To me it is life in the raw, wild and bare. It is a life in which you must meet men who live in wild countries, lead hard lives and sometimes are forced to commit harsh deeds. You will find cattlemen and cattle thieves.

"Your father used to say there were honest men on the plains raising cattle, and crooks in the hills raising hell. I guess he knew what he was doing when he demanded that I send you into that atmosphere upon your eighteenth birthday. I am not questioning his judgment, but I do not pretend to approve of it. Nor do I pretend to admire such a life nor understand its fascination for anybody. But your father said men lived there, deep in the currents, while I only drifted along on the surface. Perhaps. I do not see fit to argue the point.

"It is merely that I took an oath to send you, and I am keeping that oath. You will understand now why I had you taught to shoot and ride so well that few men could prove your superior. It is a hard life to which you go. To a life that may teach you strange viewpoints and odd angles on the varying values of relative rights and wrongs. I believe you can take care of yourself. Every six months you are to write me how you fare. I will send you money every six months. When you need more than I send, write for it. Are you ready to go?"

"Not ready—eager!" Jay stood very straight.

Again Orme smiled, but this time there was light in the smile. *She* would have said that. "As I have tried to equip you in spirit and ability to meet your future, I wish to equip you in appearance so that you will blend with your surroundings and not know from the outset the handicap of being out of tone. Your father wore this outfit when he punched cows, as he called it, on the Whiskey Flask ranch in the Bitter Roots in Montana. It will not last long. It is old, but you can refurnish yourself any time.

"I advise you to take a line of travel that will lead you continually through the cattle country. I will give you Pilgrim, the best horse I have. Go across into Texas, through New Mexico and Arizona to Utah, then on through Idaho to Montana. That will take you on a journey of close to three thousand miles, and if you wish to stop at the Iron Kettle before you return to meet your father, do so. But remember you have seven years to get there. Take your journey slowly and learn as you go. It is not in my agreement with your father that I should ask you to choose no permanent companion, to travel alone. I do not ask it. I do not even advise it. But I approve of it.

"You may take those things now, and dress."

For a moment Jay stood motionless, staring down at the chair, thinking strange thoughts. Then he abruptly stooped, gathered up his father's cowboy paraphernalia and strode from the room.

Chapter VII

MAMMY CINDY, SEERESS

An hour afterward Jay rode Pilgrim down the lane. As he had left the house to go to the barn for his horse, Orme, passing him in the hall, had uttered a casual, "Well, take care of yourself, Jay." He never knew that Orme had waited restlessly in an adjoining room, listening for his footsteps, in order to achieve that casual farewell. Now, as he drew opposite the house, he half halted Pilgrim, turning in the saddle to gaze at the silent and shadowed old building, but Orme's face did not show at any window. Inarticulately Jay understood that Orme shrank from goodbyes.

Jay nudged Pilgrim with his knees and rode on down the lane, eyes straight ahead. Not once did he look back. But at the gate, between the stone pillars, he found two who waited for him, to speak the goodbye Orme could not give. Old Eros, his wooly mop white as cotton, stood by Mammy Cindy. Her black face was somber and stern, and her hands were hidden under her apron. He drew Pilgrim to a stop, gazing down at the two old negroes, feeling a vague regret. He had become fond of Eros and Cindy. Eros shuffled toward him.

"Jes' come to see yo' off, young Massa." Eros's

voice was muffled. He hesitated, stumbled, and finished hurriedly. "Ah—goodbye, suh. Ah hopes yo' git along well. Goodbye, suh."

And without waiting for any answer, he turned and shuffled back up the lane. Mammy Cindy withdrew her hands from under her apron, stepped close to Pilgrim's side. Jay felt a quickening sense of expectancy as he glanced down at her.

"What is it, Mammy?"

"Massa Jay—" Cindy came even closer, her voice lowered. "It ain't right nohow, yo' startin' out thisaway, knowin' nothin'. Massa Jason loves yo' a heap, but he gib his word. Ah done gib mah word, too, and Ah ain't gwine back on it. Ah kain't break mah word to Massa Jason, or to yo' daddy and yo' mammy, but Ah's got to gib yo' a word of warnin'. Did Massa Jason say nothin' to yo' about airy fella named Costa, honey?"

"Costa? No." Jay watched the old negress closely. "Costa what?"

"Guido Costa, Massa Jay. Costa's his last name. Or was. He's daid. But he's got a brother some place, and yo' kain't travel around without runnin' into him. This old world don't work thataway, nohow. Yo's sho' gwine see that man. And honey—Ah sees trouble." The old black face was tense with anxiety and concern. "It's all dark. Trouble, and shootin', and mysterious goin's on. Yo' take care o' yo'se'f!"

Jay nodded, slowly, his red-brown eyes on Mammy Cindy's face. Her shining black eyes were hard and intent, like the trance-fixed eyes of a seeress. Jay wasn't inclined to attach any importance to her words. But he mustn't let her see that he received her warning lightly. Yet she noted the half smile around his eyes, and she grew slightly excited.

"Trouble! Ah knows mo' than yo', and Massa Jason knows mo' than me, but dey's a lot that nobody knows exceptin' the good Lawd. But Ah sees things. And don't yo' laugh at me! A gal with yallah hair like ripe co'n in the moonlight and with big grey eyes—yo's gwine love dat gal, but yo' look out! She's gwine bring yo' mo' trouble if yo' don't. But, please, Massa Jay, most yo' look out fo' Costa's brother."

She whirled away without a backward look. She had made her gift, warning, the outpouring of her spirit. She could do no more. Jay glanced after her, still half smiling, passed between the gate posts and went from sight down the street. It might, as Orme had predicted, be far in the future. It might even encompass those seven years. But Jay knew that he was on his way back to the Iron Kettle.

Chapter VIII

THE BEGINNING OF A JOURNEY

A youth in cowpuncher's garb stopped at a ranch in Texas and offered to pay for his board and lodging over night. The grizzled puncher he addressed stared at him, told the youth to put up his horse in the barn, and stood looking after him as though he discerned something about the stranger not at all congruous with his dress. Before the evening was half over, the boys in the bunkhouse, regarding him curiously, were hazarding many a secret guess concerning the youth with the broad muscular figure and with the odd glow in his red-brown eyes.

Jay sensed it sharply, sensed the arm's length attitude under their distant courtesy. It made him uneasy. He wanted to join in their conversation, to blend with their atmosphere, to be one of them. But their very efforts to be excessively polite told him tacitly that he did not belong, in their judgment, and that it was useless for him to pretend that he did. He couldn't understand by what act or actions, nor by what words, he had set himself apart, had built up between him and them an invisible barrier that he could not pass. Ill at ease and constrained, he sat down on the foot of the bunk that had been assigned him, watching the boys in envious silence.

A long lean fellow, sitting by a table and reading a magazine, looked across at him with a glance of covert speculation, and ventured a question intended to draw Jay out.

"Where you been workin', stranger?"

Jay smiled, deprecatingly, eagerly. "Well, to tell you the truth, I haven't been working. My uncle brought me up, on his place east of here. My father used to be a cowpuncher years ago, and he wanted me to be one also, because he thought that was a good life for a man. My uncle gave me dad's old outfit and sent me out to learn to be a cowboy. This is my first stop."

The puncher threw back his head and laughed, slapped his magazine down on the table, and bent on Jay a friendly grin. "That explains it. You see, kid, we knew there was something just not regular about you, but we couldn't figure out just what it was. This is the first place you've stopped, eh? Well, you struck it lucky. If you want to learn to be a cowboy, you couldn't have done nothing better for yourself as a beginning than stop at the Roman Six ranch. You always stick to the truth like that, kid, and you won't have no trouble learnin' to be a cowpuncher, or anything else in this world."

Jay felt the sudden subtle change in the whole atmosphere. Magically, the distant courtesy and coolness had vanished. In its place, as magically, was born warmth and comradeship and railing jeers that told him they had opened the doors and taken him in. He was silent, striving to place the psychological cause of that effect. He looked up at a grizzled old puncher sitting on the bunk next him smoking in silence. It was the same puncher who had first spoken to him when he arrived.

"What's on your chest, kid?" the old puncher asked, noting the puzzled look in Jay's eyes.

"I don't just know," Jay answered. "But your attitude toward me is changed. Is it simply because I told the truth? I couldn't have done differently."

"Oh, yes you could," the old puncher contradicted dryly. "You could have claimed you'd been workin' on some other ranch. You could have pretended to be a regular cow nurse—when we knew damn well you wasn't."

Jay smiled broadly. He had had his first lesson in the cowpunchers' world. It was not what a man pretended to be, and not what he seemed to be, that counted with these fellows. What a man was, that made the difference, and a man would have to prove what he was. He turned to the grizzled old puncher.

"Do you think I could get a job here?" he asked.

"Well, seeing as I'm the foreman, I reckon I could guess at it. My name's Jefferson. The boys call me Jeff. After you've been around the Roman

Six for a few months you'll get the rough edges rubbed off. What did you say your name was?"

"I don't know." Jay grinned ruefully. "Only that my first name's Jay. And I can't explain that. But there's no dishonor in it. My mother's dead and I can't remember my father much. I suppose I have a right to *take* a name, in that case, haven't I?"

"You sure have," Jeff responded heartily. "Names ain't worth a hoot in hell anyway unless the man that wears 'em is a real hombre." His face crinkled in a wide smile. "What did you say your name was?"

A somber silence had fallen over the bunkhouse, silence of sympathetic understanding. The silence of men startled and confounded at the unusual circumstances of finding a nameless boy in their midst. Their covert glances appraised him. Jay thought swiftly. A name he must have, but how to choose it?

He realized suddenly that other men's names were other men's names. Not his. He could not attach himself to another man's name. He must find something that directly applied to him. And abruptly he answered Jeff.

"I guess we'll say it's Malo." He grinned broadly. "I used to have a burning ambition to be a bad man, and I've heard that Malo is Spanish for bad."

Laughter arose around him at his sally. "All right," the foreman replied. "Malo it is. And by the way, Malo, there's one thing I know you can do. I saw you ride in, and you ride as though you'd been sitting a hoss for the last ten years. That's a good start toward being a cowpuncher. What about them smoke wagons you're totin'? I reckon, seeing that it's you totin' 'em, they ain't no bluff."

Jay gazed at him, savoring that last remark. If it was he carrying the guns, Jeff reckoned they were no bluff. The beginning of a reputation.

So Jay Malo came to the Roman Six in Texas. He stayed there three months. When he left, as Jeff had predicted, the rough edges were worn off. At the next ranch where he stopped the boys would not know him instantly as a tenderfoot ignorant of the ways of the range. He had learned the fundamental reasons for the little written laws and the great unwritten laws which had built up the traditions of which he was to become a part.

At that next ranch, two days' journey beyond the Roman Six, he rode in like a man at home, took his place—and did not offer to pay for his board and lodging.

He had now a card of recommendation, figuratively speaking. He had been working on the Roman Six. By virtue of what he had learned there he was able to conduct himself like a cowboy, as well as look like one.

And so, to the Upset Anchor ranch there came Jay Malo, late of the Roman Six.

When Jay departed from the Upset Anchor it was nearly fall and the time of the roundup. As he jogged along in the hot sun he reflected on the time that had passed since he had left his uncle's home in Louisiana. Five months, and he wasn't halfway across Texas. He began to understand how it might take those seven years to reach the Iron Kettle. He had a long, long way to go.

The next afternoon he and Pilgrim arrived at the Broken Wheel ranch. Jay didn't like the place. So he moved on. He rode on steadily for five days. This long jump brought him to the Double K ranch in New Mexico. At the Double K they put Jay on for the roundup. When the fall roundup was ended, his first six months were up.

It was time to write to Orme, he must find something to say. He found this much:

> Dear Uncle Jason:
>
> The first six months are over. I have gotten only as far as New Mexico. I have worked on four different ranches. I am teaching Pilgrim to be a cowhorse, and he takes to it with an ease that is a credit to him. I don't need any money. Save it till I do. Jay.

The next day Jay and the big brown horse hit the trail again. By the spring roundup he had reached southern Arizona. The country was already beginning to swelter in the coming heat. Along toward the close of his stay at that ranch he sat outside of the barn in the coolest place he could find, and his attention was caught by the sound of someone singing. He had just come from his evening meal, and though the evening was waning the setting sun was still making itself felt.

Malo leaned forward to glance toward the corrals from whence the sound of singing came. He saw Michelo, the Mexican roustabout, warbling lustily as he sat by a corral fence weaving a rawhide lariat. It was not solely the fact that Michelo was singing. The thing that had riveted Jay's interest was two words recurring in the song. The words *malo hombre.* Jay got to his feet and walked over to the corral.

"Say, Mike, what in the devil are you singing?" he asked. "Sounds like a pretty good song. Let's have it again." Michelo grinned broadly. He raised his voice with gusto and began at the beginning.

> "Oh, there was a malo hombre down
> south
> Rode a fire eatin' bronc and packed a six-
> foot gun.
> All he had to do was spread his face and
> yawn—
> Like this—

And Lordy how the folks would run!
He could battle like a cattymount and
  bella like a bull,
All the bandits on the border were afraid
  of he.
Nitric acid was his whiskey, rattlesnakes
  his meat,
And that malo hombre, fella, was me—
Like hell!
Yeh, that mucho malo hombre was me."

Jay chuckled and immediately demanded that Michelo should sing the rest of it. But the Mexican spread his hands, shrugged and shook his head.

"Thass all, Senor. Ees no more. Maybe you like to learn it. Malo, thass your name. Maybe your song, no?"

Jay's answer was a request that Michelo teach him the single stanza.

Jay had learned that he had a voice. The other cowboys were singing to the cattle half of the time. He had got into the habit as a matter of course. It was a tenor voice high and clear, with that slightly throaty quality which gives to voices of that type a noticeably plaintive intonation. And in something like a half hour after he had approached Michelo, the throaty tenor rose in the dusk, singing the *malo hombre* song, as Jay walked across the yard to the bunkhouse.

The roundup being over, he decided to move on again. He stopped next at a ranch in middle Arizona. He never afterward remembered the brand of that ranch. Everybody called it Charley's ranch. On Charley's ranch Malo decided to settle until the worst of the heat was over.

One evening in the bunkhouse, a couple of punchers entered arguing volubly about something.

One of them was a small dark man with the quick temper and impulsiveness of his type, Safaro Latizzo. Joe Ulmar, the puncher who accompanied him, had purchased a new gun, and the two of them were discussing its merits. Ulmar displayed the gun pridefully, and the rest of the boys crowded around to have a look at it. Guns were the subject of conversation for the remainder of the evening.

In the morning after breakfast, Ulmar brought out his new gun and suggested that they go down to the horse pasture and give it a try. Glad of any excuse for action, it being Sunday, the boys trooped after him as he led the way. They arrived at the horse pasture, and Ulmar sought a target.

He found a little celluloid rosette that had dropped off somebody's bridle, picked up the little disc and set it against the fence post near the top, catching it under a sliver to prevent its falling. Then he backed off some forty-odd feet and aimed at it with the new gun. The gun roared, but no mar appeared upon the little red disc. A bullet hole showed in the post an inch above it. "She shoots high," Ulmar remarked, turned to the puncher standing a few paces from him, and extended the gun. "Want to try her, Jess?"

From then on, the trial of the new gun became a free-for-all target shoot. Malo looked on smiling. Ulmar turned to him abruptly.

"What's the matter with them two smoke wagons of yours, Jay? Ain't they workin'?"

"Oh, I guess so. But you fellows have ruined the target."

"Jay." Latizzo stepped close and spoke in a loud whisper, in a mock confidential aside, intended for everyone's ears. "Toss a dollar. I don't believe these guys ever saw any real shooting. Go ahead, toss a dollar and show them something."

Malo shoved his hand into his pocket and drew out a silver dollar. He stepped back a few paces and tossed the dollar into the air. Before it had started down toward the earth, his hands flashed to his guns. The Colts roared almost together. The dollar bounced back into the air and bounded to the earth. Latizzo went at a run to pick it up, brought it back and displayed it excitedly.

The boys crowded around to look. The dollar was bent almost double, and the two dents caused by the bullets were side by side on the metal. Latizzo turned to Malo.

"I'll give you a good one for it when payday comes, Jay. I want to keep this."

"Keep it and welcome, Saff," Malo answered, "I've got another one just like it."

As the boys turned back toward the ranch buildings, Latizzo laid a hand on Malo's arm and spoke to him in an undertone.

"Look who's here, Jay."

Two men were standing in the lane beyond the barn. One of them was Charley, the owner of the ranch. The other was a ruddy faced man Malo had not seen before. His long mustache, now a golden grey, had once been fiery red. The short curling beard, and the thick waving hair showing under the hat shoved back from his forehead, matched it in shade and tone.

Malo turned to his companion inquiringly. "Who is it, Saff?"

"Sheriff Reed Bolton, from Globe," Latizzo explained. "Must be something doing in Gila County."

Charley glanced up as the two boys came toward him, and his gaze intensified as it rested on Latizzo. "Come over here, Saff," he said tersely. "Reed's got a job for you. Clint Fess is on the rampage again. Reed's goin' after him. He wants a good gunman to take along, and I reckon you're about the fastest man I've got."

"Begging your pardon, boss, I am not," Latizzo refuted, and pointed to the puncher at his side.

"Jay, here, is the fastest thing on wheels. If you want somebody that can beat both you and Clint Fess to the draw, Sheriff, Jay's it." He added hastily, "Not that I won't be glad to go, if you want me."

Reed Bolton flashed a swift survey from one young puncher to the other. "Well, I tell you how it is, Saff. I only want one man. This boy has more heft than you." His eyes bored into Malo's. "You traveling my way?"

"Wait till I get my horse," Malo answered, turned on his heel and strode toward the barn.

Bolton looked after him rather dubiously. "Seems like pretty much of a boy, Saff."

Latizzo smiled. "We've just been down to the horse pasture having a little target practice. Jay tossed up a dollar and took a crack at it with both guns. And he drew after the dollar was in the air. Here's the dollar." Latizzo held out in his palm the battered coin. A dry little smile of satisfaction lit the sheriff's face. He glanced up at the sound of a horse's hoofs, to see Pilgrim coming toward him, Malo sitting erect and alert in the saddle. Latizzo thrust the dollar into his pocket, and the sheriff turned to remount his horse.

As Malo drew alongside, the sheriff turned his horse, and the two passed down the lane together and turned into the road.

"Well, we sure got our work laid out for us,

son," the sheriff remarked. "You ever gone gunning for a man before?"

"No." Malo stared straight between Pilgrim's ears. "This is my first job of the kind."

"Well, properly speaking, Clint Fess ain't no man." Bolton's voice was hard, and the grey eyes under the cinnamon-grey brows grew cold. "He's a low-down killer of the meanest kind. He's been clutterin' up the country for years."

"Why don't somebody get him, then?" Malo asked.

"Get him!" Bolton echoed, with a short laugh. "He killed both of the sheriffs before me, when they went after him. And he may kill me. That's why you're along. That's the only job you've got, son. If Clint Fess gets me, you get him! I reckon you can. Saff showed me that dollar."

Malo looked sharply into the grim old face. "I have never yet shot at a man, Mr Bolton," he said quietly. "But if I should need to, I can't see why he'd be any harder to hit than a dollar."

Chapter IX

BEFORE DAWN

Malo and Bolton spent the night in the open and were on their way at seven thirty in the morning. The day was torrid, but they maintained a steady pace. They spent that second night under a pine tree, and the morning of the second day saw them on their way again.

Shortly after noon they arrived at the edge of the timber and saw ahead of them a grass-grown lane leading to a house a quarter of a mile beyond, the dwelling of Clint Fess. It was a one-story log cabin built in a thin grove of scrub oak and pine. A hundred yards beyond the cabin was a long bunkhouse. The lane leading to the cabin was enclosed by a rail fence, into which a gate was set opposite the building. A few yards past the gate, between it and the cabin, stood a small smokehouse. On one side of the lane lay a wide field and on the other side was a pasture. There was no cover between the forest and the house. Bolton drew on the reins and turned to Malo.

"Fess is the kind that'll shoot from the brush, Malo. It's plumb suicide to walk up on a man that shoots from ambush. We'll just cache ourselves back here where we can watch the lane. After dark we'll wade in."

They backed their horses farther into the trees, dismounted and stretched themselves on the ground where they could command a view of the lane. The sun went down and the dusk deepened to night. But no light showed, either in the log cabin or in the bunkhouse behind it.

"He sure is there, maybe hid out in that smoke-house," Bolton commented. "And he's taking no chances. Neither are we." He gestured toward the lane.

A full moon had risen early above the horizon. The long lane leading to the outlaw's cabin was flooded with its light. Anyone going down that lane would be rendered a fair target from cabin or bunkhouse. Malo answered significantly:

"It's always pretty dark just before dawn, Sheriff."

"Yeh," Bolton nodded. "Just what I was thinking."

They shifted their position under the trees cautiously. At last the dark hour came. Gradually the light faded out of the sky, the moon was gone and a black blanket seemed to have been dropped over the earth. With a sigh of relief Bolton got to his feet and felt his way to the fence enclosing the lane, Malo close at his side. It was so dark that even the stars were veiled by what seemed to be a black mist, but they advanced steadily, guiding themselves by the rail fence.

They came finally to the gate set into the fence and knew they were opposite the grove. There they halted and Malo felt the sheriff's groping touch on his arm. Then he felt the cinnamon-grey mustache against his cheek, and heard the almost soundless voice of Bolton in his ear.

"We'll slide down the lane about ten feet and climb over the fence."

He held Malo's arm as he turned back down the lane. After they had gone several paces, Bolton stopped him, pulled his head down and again whispered in his ear.

"I'll go first. You're my ace in the hole. Stand right here till I signal you to come over—with both guns ready."

Bolton went over the fence, cautiously testing every step, every foothold, as he climbed the rails. Malo waited tensely. Not a sound came to his ears. The sheriff was moving slowly, as silent as the night about him. The next thing Malo knew, he felt Bolton's hand reach over the top rail, grope for him and tug on his sleeve. He followed the sheriff into the yard. They advanced slowly and soundlessly for some forty feet. There Bolton ran into a tree, turned aside and went on. Another ten feet brought them up against the log wall of the house.

Bolton followed the wall, still guiding Malo by his hold on his sleeve. They arrived at the porch and halted again. Bolton turned and walked directly toward the fence for about twenty feet, still drawing Malo with him. There he stopped again and drew Malo's head down to whisper in his ear.

"Follow in the direction I am pointing. Go straight that way about five paces and stop. I'm going to draw their fire. You're not to fire till you know I'm hit. All right, go ahead."

Malo raised a hand, groping in the dark, and found the sheriff's arm pointing slightly backward toward the fence. He turned and noiselessly walked that way exactly five paces. As he stopped and turned to face back toward the sheriff, Bolton's gun crashed loudly into the silence and spat fire in the dark.

Over by the gate a smothered curse gave evidence of the fact that a guard was there, and that they had passed him by their maneuver. In the same breath with his curse, the guard fired at the flash of the sheriff's gun. But Bolton had already dropped flat to his belly, and the guard's bullet whined harmlessly over his head. The sheriff's gun spoke again, sharply, aimed toward the flash the guard's gun had made. A pained grunt and the thud of a falling body told Malo that the sheriff had scored.

In the same instant the door of the house burst open, and five men, invisible in the deep shadows of the night, came boiling out of the house and down the steps. Malo and Bolton knew they had emerged as surely as though they had seen them. They heard the door creak, and the thud of heels, crossing the porch and descending the steps. Malo dropped swiftly to the ground, both guns drawn.

Bolton had raised his Colt high, the full length of his arm, and fired in the direction of the men who had come from the house. At that angle the shot appeared to come from a man standing. The flash of fire spurted at about the height it would appear had a man fired it from his hip. The sheriff jerked back his arm, but before he had it down the deafening crash of six guns spewed fire and lead into the air. They were, as Bolton had planned they should be, aimed slightly above the fire from his own gun. The bullets went over his head like a flock of bees, a good two feet above his level. The roar of Bolton's gun almost blended with the crash of the others, as he fired his three remaining shots as rapidly as he could pull the trigger.

One of the outlaws cursed loudly, and the stumbling thud of falling bodies told Malo that each of those three bullets had taken their toll. But the two remaining men had now got the sheriff's position. Three guns spat their venomous reply. Bolton felt a sear as though a white-hot iron had been drawn down his body. One bullet thudded into the ground beyond him. The other struck his head, and he groaned with the shock as his empty gun fell from his fingers.

Malo heard him. The sheriff was hit. Before the sputtering sparks had died from those last three shots, Malo sent two bullets toward the outlaws. There was a curse and a grunt. One of the men fell. As Malo fired, he had rolled more than a foot to the right. Instantaneous answer came from the one remaining outlaw, the sole one of them who had two guns. He had thrown himself flat. Two bullets whizzed by Malo, cutting through the space to his left, where he had lain but an instant before. His own guns answered. This time there was no vindictive reply. Nothing but the slight sound of a gun falling onto the board walk.

With straining ears, Malo waited in motionless alertness. But no further sound came.

Malo loaded his guns again, got cautiously to his feet and walked slowly through the blackness of the night in the direction of the sheriff's breathing. He could not be certain. Clint Fess was sly enough to be lying there unharmed, waiting the opportunity of a sure shot.

Malo paused, thinking. He must take care of Bolton's wounds, and he needed water. The only place he knew to find it around there was in the house. The best way of caring for the sheriff was to get him into the house, anyway. And he couldn't do a thing for him till he had light. Neither did he dare attempt to go in the house until he had ascertained that Clint Fess and his men were incapacitated for making any further trouble.

He bent close to Bolton. "Take it as easy as you can and wait a minute, Mr Bolton. I'm going to have a look around."

He rose, carefully felt his way around the sheriff's prone body and toward the house. Light was an immediate necessity. He dared not wait for dawn to break. Bolton might die during the waiting. He had no idea how badly he was hurt. Fess might be alive and maneuver to succeed in getting them both. Light and action both were necessary. Malo quickened his steps as much as he dared. He reached the house, followed around it and arrived at the opposite corner of the front. There he turned and started in the direction in which he calculated the smokehouse to be, guiding himself by its position between cabin and gate.

He arrived unexpectedly at the rail fence. He had missed the smokehouse. He swerved and turned up the fence for some six paces, then started back toward the cabin again. He had gone but a little distance when he became aware of a faint odor in the air. The scent of burned wood, and stale meat combined with the raw pungency of mouldering potatoes. The smokehouse.

Malo moved straight toward the odor and in another moment had stumbled against the shake wall of the small building. He felt his way around it till he found the plank door, shoved it open, stepped inside and, keeping close to the wall, made a complete round of the interior, his guns held ahead of him ready to go into action on the first sign of someone hidden in the smokehouse. But they touched nothing and he came again to the open door satisfied. No one was there.

He pulled the door shut, holstered his right gun and struck a match. The building was composed of thin shakes laid over a light framework of rough lumber. Both lumber and shakes were very old, seasoned and tinder dry, and splintered cracks showed here and there between the shakes. He leaned down and thrust the burning match between two ragged shakes into a narrow crack. The thin shake crackled and burst alive with fire all along its edge. Malo rose to his height, drew his other gun and stepped to the door, slipped out and closed it behind him.

Surer of his bearings now, he made his way back to the cabin, quickly and noiselessly, rounded it and found the sheriff.

He holstered both his guns, picked up the sheriff in his arms, and made his way back to the corner of the house. There he placed the elder man upon the ground and stood by him, guns again drawn. Mystified, Bolton asked what it was all about, and Malo told him to look over toward the gate. The sheriff turned his head and looked about in the blackness. Between cabin and gate a dull red glow was rising. The glow rose rapidly to a brighter red as the fire made progress. The flames burst through the roof and lurid yellow light threw its illumination over the yard, till within a very few moments there was good visibility from the cabin to the old rail fence. Five motionless bodies lay sprawled before the house. Malo's gaze moved to the gate. The rising light picked out the huddled lifeless body of the guard. Satisfied, Malo went into the house and made a cautious survey of it. No one was within. Having made certain of that, he struck a match: its brief flicker showed him a kerosene lamp sitting on a homemade table. He lit the lamp, and hurried back to the sheriff. It was a short journey to the steps and into the house, and in a few moments Malo had the wounded man in the chair close to the table in the glow of the lamp. For the first time he got sight of the wound in Bolton's head.

Since the sheriff had been lying down when he was hit, the bullet had gone through his hat brim, furrowed his cheek, sunk into his jaw bone and lodged. The drooping mustache and curling beard were wet with blood. The stern old face was white and the grey eyes haggard with dizziness and pain.

"Are you hit anywhere else?" Malo inquired with quick concern.

"Yes. Scored from my belly to my thigh. But

that one isn't bad. It's this jaw wound that's bothering me. You've got to get busy and dig that bullet out. If you don't there'll be hell to pay."

"I? I couldn't do that!" Malo protested, startled. "I don't know the first thing about surgery. I have no instruments."

"You don't have to know nothing, and you don't have to have no instruments," Bolton answered. "Just rustle around in Clint's kitchen, find something with a sharp point on it, and get to work."

"But—" Malo's face blanched. "I can't do it, I tell you. It would hurt like the devil. I'll get you to a doctor—"

"Don't argue," Bolton cut in wearily. "You've *got* to do it. The nearest doctor's nearly two hundred miles away. Before you could get me to him gangrene might set in. Can't take the chance. Don't make me talk so much, son. It's damn painful. Just get busy."

Malo nodded and turned away. The glow in the red-brown eyes was only a ghastly glimmer. He had never seen dead and wounded human beings before. He knew nothing about wounds nor the treatment of them. But one word the sheriff had spoken was stronger than his own shrinking. Gangrene! He thought of those long miles to reach the doctor, traveling in the hot sun. Gangrene.

His face was white and his eyes black, but his

step was steady as he walked into the kitchen. He found another lamp on the window sill, lit it and surveyed the room. A rusted old stove stood in one corner. By it lay a scattered heap of wood and kindling. Against the wall stood a crude bench: on it was a pail half filled with water. By the pail was a tin basin. Under the bench on the floor was a small wooden box containing a heterogenous collection of tools, bolts, harness thread and small junk. Malo drew the box out into the light.

Hasty rummaging brought to view an awl and a pair of small long-nosed pincers. Malo took awl and pincers, and got to his feet. Lifting the pail, he poured some of the water into the tin basin, dropped awl and pincers into the basin, and carried pail and basin to the stove. He set the receptacles on the stove and turned to the wood and kindling. In little time he had a fire roaring in the stove. Then he went into the adjoining room.

He steeled himself, bent over the sheriff and raised a hand to the wound. The bullet was easily discerned. By drawing aside the severed flesh he could see the black blot it made. He turned away again to the kitchen, with a sick feeling somewhere in the pit of his stomach. The little stove was hot, red hot in places, and the water in the pail was steaming. The smaller amount in the basin had already begun to boil. Malo laid aside his hat and pulled his flannel shirt over his head.

From his body he drew his clean linen undershirt. He replaced the flannel shirt and ripped the linen undershirt to strips, dropping the strips into the pail of water.

From the boiling water in the basin he fished out the sterilized awl and pincers. With a strip of the linen, he carried the tools into the other room, laid the linen strip on the table and placed the instruments upon it.

Then, with a set and colorless face, he picked up the awl. Carefully he spread the wound and drew the curling beard out of his way. With the awl he tested the position of the bullet. He found the lead slug fairly firmly lodged. He felt around it until he had ascertained by what set of grip he could obtain hold on it. He laid the awl back upon the linen strip and picked up the pincers. The sick feeling was again at the pit of his stomach, stronger than before, and cold sweat had started all over his body. But he dared make no least pause, lest his desperate courage desert him. With that one harsh word—*gangrene*—he drove himself on.

He inserted the pincers into the wound, located the bullet and obtained a firm hold on it.

"Hold steady, Sheriff." His voice was harsh with repression.

Bolton's only answer was to close his eyes and set himself to endure. The next moment or two remained ever after a black nightmare for Jay

Malo. He did not know exactly what he did. He only knew that he had moved somehow, that the sheriff had groaned, and that he had suddenly found himself staring at the extracted bullet in the pincers. He wheeled and fairly ran into the kitchen. All the water was boiling now. He thrust the tips of the pincers into the pail and drew out strips of the sterilized linen. He rushed back to the sheriff, his whole body wet with sweat, but some of the sick feeling was gone.

Bolton opened his eyes and smiled. "When you get it washed out, Malo, pour some of that boilin' water in it to cauterize it."

Malo made no demur. He was hardened to anything now. He washed the wound, brought another strip from the pail and allowed the scalding hot water to drip into the wound. He cleaned the curling beard, packed and dressed the wound with efficient speed. Then he turned his attention to the body wound. He found it merely a long score, less than a half inch deep, running from Bolton's left breast to his thigh. He cleansed it thoroughly, and hurried into the kitchen again. In one corner stood a barrel with a small quantity of flour in the bottom. He caught up double handfuls of the flour, hurried back and plastered the flour thickly over the long score. When he had the bleeding quite stanched, he aided the sheriff to replace his clothing.

"Man, you're a record breaker for speed!"

Bolton said, with a smile. "I feel almost as good as new. Ain't dizzy at all no more."

Malo nodded soberly. Out of the daze of the last grisly hour, he realized something had happened to him. Something had gone out of him. And something had come into him. He was not as he had been. From his nausea and shock he had emerged strangely cool, calm and clear headed. What was it that had happened to him? He started as he recalled what Bolton had said. He had not called him son, nor boy, nor any appellation indicating his youth. He had said—*man.*

Chapter X

MARGARHITA

Malo returned to the ranch only to tell Charley that he was moving on. In the bunkhouse that evening, Safaro Latizzo watched from the corner of his eye as Malo went out the door. For the first time in his life the little Italian had found a man to whom his impulsive affection went out unreservedly. But that man had shown no inclination to return his emotion. Nine men out of ten would have let it rest at that, either through pride, or a male aversion to displaying their feelings. But Safaro Latizzo was the tenth man. He rose quietly from the foot of his bunk and followed Malo out of the bunkhouse.

He saw him walking in the direction of the corral beyond the barn, with his head down, apparently lost in intent thought. Latizzo strode rapidly toward the opposite side of the barn, passed the building and came out into the lane by the corral wing just as Malo approached the fence. His appearing there had all the seeming of a casual chance meeting. Hearing his footstep, Malo glanced up and paused by the fence.

"Hello there, Saff."

"H'lo, Jay." Latizzo drew closer and leaned

upon the fence post. "I hear you're leaving us tomorrow." He had no idea where Malo was going, but he hoped that insinuating suggestion might elicit that information. The hope was vain. Malo only nodded, unsmiling, and said yes. "I—sure hate to see you go," Latizzo went on. He would have given anything he possessed to have drawn from Malo an invitation to go with him. Malo's cool aloofness did not smooth the way for the Italian's stumbling tongue. Latizzo repeated, inanely; "I sure hate to see you go."

Malo said nothing. Doggedly, Latizzo tried again.

"Couldn't you manage to stay a while longer? The boys are planning to give a little blowout next week—dance and everything. Chub's sister and a lot of the girls will be over."

"No. I can't stay." Malo shook his head and his somber eyes passed over Latizzo's face. "I have a long way to go yet before I reach my objective, and I must be moving. And—I care nothing about girls. Probably, because I've never had anything to do with them."

Latizzo remained silent for a moment, wondering at Malo's mood. Then he said, curiously; "You mean to tell me you never had a girl yet?"

"I have not," Malo replied curtly, in a tone of voice which indicated that he had no wish to pursue the subject.

Latizzo straightened. After all, he could not

combat this chill reserved mood that enveloped Jay. He could not say the thing he wanted to say. He could not ask bluntly. "Where are you going? Can I go along?" Dumbly, disappointed and rebuffed, he turned away.

Malo walked slowly onward. Saff's remark concerning girls had jarred upon him. His mind reverted to the things Jason Orme had taught him. Frankly, but rather solemnly, with a kind of stern chastity, Orme had taught Jay all there was to know about life and himself. And about women. He had *not* taught him to set woman upon a pedestal and worship her as a divinity beyond reach. He had taught him, with no equivocation, that woman as woman was to be respected. That she was a human being whose rights in life and to independence were as clearly defined as man's. That she was not in any sense a lesser being of small importance specifically designed for man's interest, pleasure and desertion. The words had done their work. Jay respected women, as long as they respected themselves. When they failed to do that, he ignored them. He was quite well aware that he knew absolutely nothing about them. He had not until lately felt any curiosity concerning women. But the curiosity was there, latent, and that one question of Latizzo's had prodded it into the first stirrings of life. It was not so much the question itself that had flicked him as it was the astounded incredulity with which Saff had said,

"You mean to tell me you never had a girl yet?"

He paused beyond the corral. He thought of what Cindy had said—a girl with yellow hair, with hair like ripe corn in the moonlight. He had never seen ripe corn in the moonlight. He felt a sudden warming in his blood as there came before his sight a vague vision of a nebulous feminine face with grey eyes shadowed under pale yellow hair. He flushed unconsciously, turned on his heel and started briskly toward the bunkhouse.

The next morning he was up early, making preparations for his leave taking. He left the ranch as Latizzo and the other boys were going to work.

The boys called sociable farewells as he rode away from the barn, but Latizzo followed him for several yards and leaned upon the fence.

"Say, Jay." Latizzo made one last effort to keep some bond remaining between him and this man who had set his face the other way. "You might drop a fellow a line."

"I won't promise." Malo looked back over his shoulder, unsmiling. "I'm not much of a letter writer, Saff. But if I'm ever back in this territory I'll be sure to look you up."

"Yeh. Do that. Well, I got to get to work." Defeated, Latizzo turned from the fence as Malo rode down the dusty road. He knew no letter would ever come. And Malo rode toward Montana.

• • •

Days later, he entered a range of hills and passed through a low flat gulch, to find himself facing a party of men. There were seven of them, and they had emerged unexpectedly from a knot of trees which had been within his range of vision for the last fifteen minutes. Their faces were weary and their eyes were hard. They were armed to the hilt and their horses showed evidence of hard riding.

The middle-aged dark-haired man riding in the lead wore a sheriff's star. His deep keen eyes played swiftly over Malo.

"How are you, stranger?" The officer's eyes probed his gaze. "May I ask who you are and where you are going?"

"You certainly may. I am Jay Malo, and I am bound for the Iron Kettle ranch."

"Never heard of it. Stranger in this territory, aren't you?" The sheriff studied a moment after he had received Malo's confirming nod in answer to that question. He went on abruptly; "I'm Marcus Whitney. On the trail of Motch Gleason. Have you seen or heard anything of him?"

"Who's Motch Gleason?" Malo asked.

In reply, Whitney drew from his pocket a printed dodger, pointing to the likeness of a man on the sheet as he passed it over to Malo. It informed the reader that Motch Gleason, six feet four inches tall, with black hair and black eyes, weighing a hundred and sixty pounds, was wanted by the law for robbery and murder. The only distinguishing mark upon him was a marred left ear; the lower half of the ear had been sliced off in some brawl. To anyone who brought him in, or gave information by which he was captured, alive or dead, a thousand dollars would be paid. Malo smiled as he finished reading the dodger and returned it to Whitney.

"I haven't seen anything of such a bean pole as that, Sheriff. Is he in this territory?"

"He has been, very lately. We've been riding the hills for two days, but it looks like we'd have to give it up and conclude that he's made another slick getaway. If you should happen to run into him, or any sign of him three shots fired in succession will bring some of us running. Well, I won't detain you. I want to ride that east ridge over there before dark. So long."

Malo answered with a like salutation of farewell and rode on. The afternoon had waned into evening, when he came to a spring at the base of a hill. It was a good place to camp. Shade from the low hanging sun, water and plenty of grass on the flat.

Malo halted his horses, swung out of the saddle and went to the spring to drink. Pilgrim and the pack horse thrust their noses into the cool creek. When Pilgrim had satisfied his thirst and raised his dripping muzzle from the water, Malo stepped to him and started to remove his saddle.

There was a sudden movement in the trail beyond the spring. Malo raised his head quickly and turned. A lone rider was coming toward him, from the direction in which he had been going. The newcomer rode a light buckskin, and must have come fast and far. The horse's flanks and breast were darkened with sweat.

Whatever thoughts or suspicions might have occurred to Malo at the sight of that unexpected figure approaching, were entirely swept into the background by astonishment. The stranger was a girl. She halted her horse across the spring and sat silent in the saddle, looking at him with veiled intentness.

Malo returned her gaze with his astonishment hidden under that cool unshakable poise he had attained back there in Clint Fess's log cabin at dawn. It was a fair face he saw, a face that had once been beautiful. Was still beautiful, to one who could not read the shifting hard light in her wide eyes. Malo saw only that the eyes were grey. That the fair face was framed by ash blonde hair, like—like ripe corn in the moonlight.

He was held silent at that abrupt recollection of Cindy's words. It was owing largely to Cindy, and to the remembrance of his own thought when he had stood alone on Charley's Ranch and gazed at the dying moon, that he saw her through a deceptive haze.

As for her, one look into his face, and she knew

him for exactly what he was. He was grist to her mill, answer to her frantic demand, (she had forgotten there is such a thing as a prayer). He was fish to her net and a tool to her scheme. Her fair face changed subtly. It was too subtle for Malo to comprehend. The grey eyes dropped a veil of deceit over their rocky gleam. To Malo it only seemed that, strangely, she took on an added beauty there before his eyes.

"Good afternoon, stranger," she said softly. "You don't belong in this part of the country, do you?"

He moved a step nearer. "No, I don't ma'am," he answered. "I'm from Louisiana. I'm on my way north. It seems to me this is a pretty wild territory for a young lady like you to be riding around alone. There's a murderous outlaw loose in this neck of the woods somewhere."

"No! Is there?" The grey eyes widened. She appeared quite startled. But she was thinking to herself—from Louisiana! On his way north! Fish to her net indeed.

"I saw the sheriff a few miles back, and he told me to be on the lookout. You'd better let me take you home, where you'll be safe from men like Motch Gleason."

"I can't go home until I get help," she explained. An anxious look crossed her face. "That's what I'm doing out here alone. I came for help."

"For help!" Malo stepped toward her quickly. "You're in trouble of some kind? Is there anything I could do?"

For a moment she remained quite still, studying him. He bore her silent scrutiny patiently, waiting for her to speak. From some Godforsaken place she coaxed a note of plaintive despair as she leaned toward him.

"Yes, I suppose you could. You see, my brother is very ill. I'm afraid to sit up with him myself. He might—he might—die!"

She really did it very well. He reached out a hand, surprised at his own boldness, and touched her arm.

"Don't worry. You needn't sit up alone with him. The delay of one night will make very little difference in my journey. I'll be only too glad to sit up with you, and to do anything I can for your brother."

She drew a breath of relief and shot a sharp glance at him. Her fish was caught. Now, to plan how best she might use him. She had not dreamed that fate could send her this particular kind of fish. She had never found fate so benevolent. She said quickly;

"Oh, there really isn't anything you can do for him. He must be kept very quiet. The doctor was insistent about it. All anyone can do is just to keep me from being alone."

"Well, I can certainly do that," Malo affirmed

heartily. “Which way do we go?” And he turned to Pilgrim to tighten the cinch he had started to loosen when she first came in sight.

“This way.” She turned her horse, as he picked up the lead rope for the pack horse and swung into the saddle. “I didn’t tell you my name. It’s Margarhita. Margarhita Panzaol.”

Malo thought that Margarhita was a perfect name for a girl with grey eyes and hair like ripe corn in the moonlight. Cindy had said that he would love the girl with yellow hair. Regarding it as a possibility, the blood crept into his face, and he stared straight ahead at the hills as they rode, lest she see that in his eyes.

Margarhita Panzaol welcomed that averted gaze. It gave her better opportunity for studying him further. She watched him covertly from the corner of her eye. Verily he was a Godsend, though she was not capable of applying so reverent a word.

She had demanded fiercely and without specification, a tool with which to jimmy the doors and windows being slowly closed to imprison her. Some vagarious power had sent her a perfect tool. But she was hardly capable of feeling any degree of gratitude. She could only plan to use him, little caring how he might suffer as a result.

And she satisfied herself that he himself was so innocent in those dark ways of which she was master that any pose she might assume would pass without arousing his suspicions. She ascertained, as she put it to herself, that some poor dub had taught him to respect women merely because they were women. And she laughed, inwardly, so that he could not see. He asked what ailed the sick brother, and she told him mournfully that it was a bad case of fever.

She saw what a profound impression she had created by that sisterly concern, so she continued to dwell upon it with telling effect. By the time they reached their objective, Malo's heart ached for her. Her helplessness touched him deeply. He was ready to take her into his arms and shield her; to hold her closely and ward off the blows of grief and bereavement, or to soften them if they must fall.

They came into sight of a small rough cabin in a grove of stunted trees, so effectually and cleverly concealed that Malo had not the least idea that a cabin was there until they were within ten feet of it. Malo unsaddled and fed the horses and followed her into the cabin. The interior had two small rooms. The door to the farther room was closed. She excused herself, saying that she must see how her brother was feeling, passed through the connecting door and shut it behind her. Malo heard her speak in a lowered tone, and heard a reply in the querulous voice of a man in pain.

When Margarhita returned, his gaze focussed sharply on her face. The fair features were white and her mouth quivered as she looked at him. Quite without his own volition Malo was across the room and had her in his arms. He had no time to consider that he was acting with temerity. He was moved solely by the grief in her eyes. She dropped her head onto his breast, and for a moment he thought she was going to cry. But she moved back and smiled up at him.

"I'm all right, but he—he *is* sick."

"You're sure there's nothing I could do?"

"Nothing. Only build me a fire in the stove. I'll get something to eat. You can find wood out in the grove."

Malo shortly had a fire going in the dilapidated kitchen stove. Margarhita lit a couple of candles, thrust them into the necks of bottles in lieu of a lamp, and set the bottles on the table. Then she moved about the room frying bacon and setting cold boiled beans to warm, while Malo sat tilted in a chair against the wall and watched her.

The evening passed into night. He kept his distance a little too rigidly to suit her purpose. She knew the efficacy of brine in a woman's eyes. It was not a difficult matter to bring the tears. She rose from the table and walked up and down the room. She paused close to Malo and looked into his face, her grey eyes brimming. He reached out a quick hand. She was past mistress in the art.

But she realized that the game was going to be

harder than she had thought, when he abruptly left her and went out to walk blindly under the stars. She waited impatiently for him to come back. He did not come. She was exasperated, angered. One of the candles burned itself out, and still he had not returned. But she heard his footsteps pass the door, come back to it, hesitate, and pass again. Well, if higher pressure was necessary, higher pressure she would apply. She began to sob audibly, in pity and anxiety for her dear brother on his bed of pain. That, she estimated, when he heard it, would be more potent than the impulse that had sent Malo from her out into the night. It was.

His hand fell upon the door latch, remained there a moment, and Malo held his breath, listening intently. No, he was not mistaken. She was sobbing aloud. He wrenched open the door and rushed to her.

It was dawn when he left her asleep and went out to roam the grove and commune with himself. And now, deliberately, he recalled all that Mammy Cindy had said. He laughed aloud. Cindy had said trouble. Trouble! He had heard before that love comes swiftly. He walked for two hours, waiting for her to waken. Then she came out of the cabin and called him.

Now she was ready to play her cards. She told him the crisis had passed. She asked him to go in with her and see her brother.

Jay Malo stepped through that connecting door and took one long look at the man who lay in the bed in that other room. He was a very tall man. So tall that he had to keep his knees doubled to prevent his feet from protruding over the foot of the bunk. He was as thin as a cadaver, and his face was almost colorless as one. His hair was black. The eyes that glanced up at Malo matched it in color. The lower half of his left ear had been shorn away by a vindictively wielded knife.

Malo went rigid. His own face paled, and the glow in his eyes blazed suddenly with a terrible light. There could be no mistake. The man on the bed was the man pictured on the dodger. In that instant he knew that the girl with yellow hair was as false and wicked as he had thought her good and true. He turned on his heel and strode out of the cabin. But she had seen his face. With a sharp word to the man on the bed, she ran after Malo. It was not to be so easy after all. She overtook Malo in the grove and caught his arm.

"Where are you going?" she demanded. "What is the matter with you?"

"Your brother—" Malo's voice was cold and his whole figure was as unresponsive as a figure of wood. The glow in his red-brown eyes was as the glitter of frost. "Are you going to attempt to deny me that he is Motch Gleason?"

"No," Margarhita stirred truth into the same brew with lies. "He is my brother, Motch Gleason.

I did not know he was an outlaw till he came to me yesterday, begging me to hide him. He was wounded. What would you have me do? He is my brother. The sheriff is headed this way. And you have got to go and meet him, and turn him back."

"You did not say Gleason was wounded," Malo replied coldly. "You said he was sick. You lied."

A dangerous light flashed in the grey eyes, but she covered it quickly. "He is wounded, and a wounded man is a sick man."

Malo said nothing. He stood before her like a man stunned, sickened, and all the exultation was dead within him. He knew that she had striven to make of him her cat's paw, knew that she had planned it from the first moment when she had come upon him down there at the spring. A devastating rage rose within him. She saw it, and her hand tightened on his rigid arm.

"You must!" she cried furiously. "You've got to. You owe me something. Do you hear that? Do you deny that?" She shook his arm in her fury. "Your love is short lived, Mr Malo. You're like all the rest of them, though I gave you credit for being different. Love and leave, eh? Well, go ahead and leave then. But you owe me a debt and you've got to pay. You've got to stop the sheriff and give Motch a chance to get away."

He stirred, like a frozen man coming to life, and the blast of his revulsion swept over her. "Love you!" His voice was like an icy wind. "I hate you. And I hate myself. I wish I'd never seen you, and I hope to God I never see you again!" Something within him retched, nauseated, at the very sight of Margarhita. She, shaken now with the fear of failure, started to speak. But he cut her short. "Keep still! Yes, damn you, I'll go. And you go back there with your cursed brother, and don't show yourself again."

She went, satisfied.

Malo saddled Pilgrim with furious haste and rode away from the cabin, shaken to the depths with his devastating rage. In his eyes a smouldering blackness almost quenched the glow. She was demanding that he shield and protect a breaker of the law. But the breaker was her brother. That was the one peg left on which to hang the least shred of excuse for her conduct—her passionate love of her brother. That thing alone saved her from his fury and drove him reluctantly to turn back Sheriff Marcus Whitney and his posse.

By late afternoon Malo neared the territory where he had last seen the sheriff. He reined Pilgrim in and fired three shots into the air. The sound of the reports died away in echoing reverberation. There was no answer. He rode on. Nearly a mile further he again fired the signal. That time instant answer came from the hill to his right, and he halted Pilgrim. The drum of galloping hoofs came down the hill, and Whitney himself, with two men behind him, rode up to a sliding halt.

"Oh, it's you?" Whitney greeted, and eagerness lit his tired eyes. "You don't mean to say you've got a line on Gleason?"

For a moment Malo hesitated. He had planned as the surest mode of procedure to say that he thought he had come upon a clue to Gleason's whereabouts, and then to lead the posse deliberately in the wrong direction. "What makes you so sure that he is still up here?" he countered.

"Well, we haven't any positive proof," Whitney answered. "Only, one of the boys thought he saw Margarhita Gleason on a ridge in these hills just a day or so ago."

"And you figure that if his sister is up here, he isn't far away?" Malo asked.

"Sister!" The sheriff stared. "She has been with him for the last three years. But she's not his sister, and she's not his wife, and she's wanted by the law as badly as he is."

Then Malo's rage burned through. The last peg was gone. His smouldering eyes turned wholly black in his white face, and the glow in them was like red fire. "Yes," he replied curtly. "I know exactly where they are. If you'll come with me I'll lead you to them."

The sheriff fired a signal to call the rest of the posse. They banded together, then, and rode into the hills straight toward the cabin that hid Motch

Gleason and his woman. Jay Malo led the way.

The sheriff walked calmly in upon them, his gun drawn. He knocked from the woman's hand the revolver she had snatched up, and handcuffed her to her fitting mate. When the woman's eyes fell upon Malo, she understood. Her curses and vile maledictions were hurled at him in a bitter hail. He only stared at her, turned Pilgrim and started away. Whitney called after him;

"Hey, Malo! You've got a thousand dollars coming!"

"I don't want it," Malo answered over his shoulder. "You fellows divide it up between you. I'm getting off cheap." He sent Pilgrim into a gallop and rode swiftly out of sight.

Chapter XI

CRUCIBLE

It came time to again write to Orme. The letter was little different from those that had gone before.

> Dear Jason:
>
> I've taken a permanent name. Malo. That's my name from now on. No news. This is a beastly letter. I'll quit.
>
> JAY.
>
> P. S. I don't need any money.

Reading that letter, Orme started and his face paled. He whispered to himself; "Malo! What a damnable trick of chance. Lord! If that boy should run into Guido Costa's brother, wearing that name!" Orme groaned and buried his head in his hands.

Up in Arizona, Malo was riding across the desert. Afar off great mesas rose before him, and though Pilgrim trudged patiently onward across the endless stretches of mesquite and alkali bottoms, the mesas never seemed to come any nearer. Malo brooded on them, watching them with somber eyes. In that vast and silent country some of the bitterness was being sweltered and burned out of his soul. He hunched against the white-hot sun, choking dust in his eyes and nose and mouth, clogging thirst furring his tongue and thickening his throat. He took a kind of fierce distorted satisfaction in the discomfort of the sun's heat, and the alkali dust that bit like acid in his eyes and throat was almost sweet. At least it was clean, he told himself savagely.

The heat mirages drifted before him, assuming their weird fantasies along the horizon. On one hand a wide flat lake glittered, stretching away toward towering hills that were as unreal as its crystal waters. Ahead of him far ranges that actually existed seemed to melt down and flatten into space. Deliberately massing chimeras dissolved into one another with steady inexorable majesty, like a slow-motion film of the beginning of the world.

He felt small and insignificant in the immensitudes around him, as though his very existence were an impertinence; felt abashed that such an insignificant atom as he should venture into the prodigious emptiness of this immense silence, where the very features of the world were changed and blended continually, as though at the whimsical fancies of some unseen omnipotent scene shifter. But it was good for him. For in that dwarfing mass of space and shifting world his feeling of unworthiness faded, the things he had so magnified in his bitterness assumed truer proportions.

For the first time since he had held in his arms the woman Margarhita, he lifted his head with the old pride and gazed into the sky above him.

In all of a year, then, nothing noteworthy came to pass, save that he wrote twice to Orme, journeyed through Utah and came into the hills of Idaho.

In the cool dusk of a spring evening, he rode down a sloping hillside and spied a campfire in the gully ahead. He was singing to himself, the stanza Mike had taught him, and the throaty tenor voice carried to the men by the campfire.

> "And that malo hombre, fella, was me.
> Like hell—
> Yes, that mucho malo hombre was me."

The men at the campfire looked up at him as he approached, grinning sociably, and one of them, a tall bearded man with chill pale eyes, called out a jovial welcome.

"Well, come on and sit in, malo hombre. This ain't no Sunday School."

Malo laughed. The men surveyed him with interest as he dismounted, loosened the cinch, heaved the heavy saddle from Pilgrim's back and relieved the pack horse of his burden.

"My name's Haney." The bearded man watched Malo closely as he said it.

Malo nodded acknowledgement of the information. "Mine is Malo, Jay for short. How far is it to the Montana line?"

"Hell, I don't know." Haney shrugged. "Not so far, I guess. Depends on who's following you. Had chuck?"

Malo said that he hadn't, and Haney told him to make himself at home and help himself. Instinctively he liked Haney. There was a hidden indefinable melancholy in the pale chill eyes. It had been Malo's intention to go in the morning. But when he went to saddle Pilgrim, he found the horse limping. A slide in the mud by the spring where Pilgrim had gone to drink explained the sprained shoulder. Malo frowned impatiently.

That settled his going for a little while. He would be compelled to wait for a few days until Pilgrim's shoulder recovered from the sprain.

Chapter XII

SHADOWS

In the next few days Malo had abundant opportunity to observe the four men with whom he was temporarily camping. The names of the other three, he learned, were Wande, Siletz and Coulone. He had been with them five days when Haney announced casually that he was going down to his ranch. He took his horse and went. He was little more than out of sight when Wande turned impressively to Malo.

"You know who that fellow is, Jay?" he asked. Malo replied that he had understood his name to be Haney. "Yes, of course," Wande agreed. "But what Haney? Well, that's Redeye Haney."

"Yes? I fear the name doesn't mean anything to me."

"Huh! Is that right?" Wande stared his astonishment. "I thought everybody in Idaho knew who Redeye Haney was. There's two thousand dollars reward on his head. Yet the sheriff ain't just stretching himself to get Redeye."

Wande paused, and Malo felt that some inquiry was expected of him. But he thought it wiser to maintain a discreet silence. Too much curiosity was dangerous. Wande repeated, meaningly;

"No, the sheriff ain't just humping himself to get Redeye. He'd have to practice about ten years to be able to beat Redeye on the draw. He knows it. Red's got quite a history. About thirteen years ago he went off his trolley and fell for a yellow-haired woman."

Malo made no remark yet something in his eyes told Wande that he had declared unqualified war on every yellow-haired woman who crossed his path. Wande went on; "Well, Red fell for this girl and married her. I guess she had a hell of a temper. Even to this day Red can't remember what they quarreled about. Some fool thing that didn't amount to a whoop in Hades. But both of them kept getting madder and madder, till she threatened to leave, and Red told her to go ahead and said she'd stay a long time before he asked her to come back. She bundled up their kid and went. Red just laughed. He figured she'd be back before night. It was such a fool quarrel. But fool quarrels is dangerous as dynamite.

"Maybe she would have come back. Hard telling. She never had no chance to come back. She and the kid took a stage across country. At one place the road runs over a pretty dangerous place, around the face of a bluff along the Little Porcupine River. As the stage went around that bluff, a big boulder dislodged from the bank above, hit the stage amidships and carried everything over into the boiling rapids; coach, passengers, driver, horses and everything.

"Some of the bodies was got back and some of them carried away in the current of the river. Red got back the body of his boy. That was about the end of things for him. It froze him. He buried the boy right and proper, then he hit for the hills. He picked us guys up here and there. We've stuck together for some time now.

"All these years he's kept the taxes paid on his ranch. He didn't want nobody moving onto the place where her and the kid used to live. But about a year ago a fellow and his wife, named Lodge, thinking the place was deserted, piled onto it and started working it. Red went down to look 'em over, intending to run them out. But this Mrs Lodge had a little kid, just about the age Red's kid would have been if he'd lived. So Red let 'em alone.

"Mary Lodge is a pretty nice woman. But Red found out that her husband is a bad egg. Got drunk every once in a while and beat up her and the boy. Finally he got to running with a couple of hard boiled guys that run a still back there in the hills. One night he come home crazy drunk, beat 'em both up something awful, broke the boy's arm and knocked her cold. That was plenty for her, and she kicked him out. He ain't showed up since, but Red keeps a pretty close eye on her and the kid."

Wande eyed Malo covertly, then added: "You understand, Jay, this Mary Lodge ain't got no idea that the friendly rancher that comes to see her and look out for her and the boy, is the outlaw Redeye Haney, with a price of two thousand dollars on his head."

Malo stiffened. Wande was trying to impress on him the size of the reward offered for Haney. Malo rose to his feet, looked Wande squarely in the eye, and replied coldly:

"All I have to say is that I hope nobody ever collects it. I'd take a supreme delight in drilling a man who tried to double-cross a fellow as square as Haney." He turned on his heel and walked away.

Malo kept to himself conspicuously for the rest of the day. He did not return to the camp until evening. As he approached the camp he heard Haney speaking.

"Well, I guess so," Haney was saying. "But what about Jay, Wande? Did you tell him what I told you to?"

"I sure did," Wande affirmed. "Told him the whole story. But I had to speak twice of that reward on your head before it got to him."

"Yes?" Haney said tensely. "What did he say then?"

Wande chuckled. "He said he hoped nobody would ever collect it. And he threatened to plug anybody that double-crossed you. He thought I was sounding him to frame you, and he ain't had nothing to do with us since."

"Good! I didn't think I could be mistaken." Haney laughed. "He's just the fellow I've been trying to find for—"

But there Haney saw Malo coming out of the trees and changed the subject abruptly. Malo joined them as casually as though he sensed nothing unusual in the air. But he was on the alert. In what fashion was he the kind of man Redeye Haney was looking for? He did not find out till the next day. After breakfast in the morning Haney offered him one of the other horses and asked him to go for a ride in the hills. They rode for perhaps a mile. Then, baldly and without preface, Redeye Haney laid his cards upon the table.

"Jay, before I became Redeye Haney, I was William Robert Blaine. Wande has saved me the trouble of relating the whole story. You know that I own a ranch, taxes paid up to date. The woman who lives there loves the place and cares for it. I want her to have it.

"But William Robert Blaine pays his taxes on that every year from another county, by mail. And nobody knows that he is the same man as Redeye Haney. I don't dare go into town and see a lawyer about fixing up that deed. My face is too well known. They'd run me in. Not that that matters so much. But I want to stick around and look after Mary. I'm all the friend she's got. I want you to go to town for me, with my power of attorney, and deed that place over to Mary Pike Lodge. What do you say?"

"You know very well I will." Malo lifted his eyes to Haney's gaze. "When do you want me to go?"

"Well, tomorrow I'd like to take you down to the ranch and introduce you to Mary. I want her to know you as a friend of mine, so that when you bring her the deed she'll know it's all right and proper. Then I don't reckon she'll see me again, although I'll stick around out of sight so I can run off that man of hers in case he shows up. You can go to town the next day. Is that all right with you?"

"Yes, certainly."

Haney got out the one word, "Thanks." Then they rode on in silence. A wind had come up. Overhead, the pine trees leaned toward each other. The wind ran over their tops with a musical soughing. Haney raised his head, listening.

"Hear that, Jay?" His upturned face was expressionless, his pale cold eyes watching the bunch-like foliage of the pines. "It makes me think of a song."

"We were wand'ring in the shadows of
the pines, my love and I,

And the wind was blowing softly from
  the sea.
When a sudden fitful darkness came
  across the summer sky,
And a shadow fell between my love and
  me.
Some hasty words were spoken, then
  almost unaware,
Hasty answers to unthinking anger led.
But my heartsick bitter longing, all my
  weeping and my prayer,
Cannot make those false and cruel words
  unsaid."

Malo listened silently, sensing the ache under Haney's brooding thoughts. A song about a useless silly quarrel that had wrought tragedy. The melody was persistent. Malo found his own brain catching and retaining the threnodic refrain. As he rolled himself into his blanket that night and dozed to sleep, he caught himself humming *In the Shadow of the Pines.*

The next day Haney and he left the camp early to call on Mary Pike Lodge. As they came in sight of the ranch house they noted that there was no sign of life about. The door was standing wide open, but even that seemed sinister. Haney scowled, dismounted and hurried toward the house, stopped short and snapped out a curse of dismay.

Mary Lodge lay stretched on the floor. Her dark brown hair was in disarray. Her eyes were closed. She had been beaten and choked into insensibility. Haney leaped toward her and caught her up in his arms. Her eyes quivered open and she gasped in relief when she saw who it was who held her.

"He—he came back last night. He beat me and took the boy. He said he'd take him where I'd never see him again. He said—he said if I sent anyone after him, or tried to get him back, he'd kill him." She struggled up in Haney's arms, gripping his shoulder with frantic hands. "He'll do it! Mr Blaine—he'll do it!"

"Not by a damn sight he won't!" Haney snapped. "You see this fellow here? Well, he's my friend, Jay Malo. Lodge won't hurt that boy. Malo and I will stop him. You straighten up and get a grip on yourself, Mary."

It took the two of them half an hour to quiet her to such an extent that they felt it safe to leave her.

Malo was scarcely in the saddle when Haney joined him, and they turned toward the camp at a long gallop. Wande, Siletz and Coulone, seated in the shade of a tree, sprang to their feet in alarm as Haney and Malo came racing into camp.

"Get your horses!" Haney commanded. "Wande, you ride the extra buckskin with the white foot. We're off to the still after Lodge. He's got the boy!"

The men whirled and rushed to their horses. As they rounded together, mounted, guns loaded, ready to ride, Haney snapped terse orders.

"He'll have taken the boy to the still. We're bringing him back. If we have to kill every damn man in the bunch—kill 'em! But the boy's got to be brought back unharmed. All ready? Then ride!"

The little band streamed over the hills, Malo and Haney in the lead. Haney's pale eyes were like white flint as they neared the whiskey still, and he raised a hand, signaling his band to halt.

They dismounted and tethered their horses, to approach the quarry afoot. They spread into a half circle around the clearing's edge, and at Haney's low spoken order concealed themselves in that position. So hidden in the edge of the trees, each man commanded a view of the dugout door.

Haney stepped toward the door. One of the men who ran the still opened the door before Haney reached it, stepped into the doorway and eyed him with a hostile, surly scowl.

"What'll you have?" he demanded. Haney replied curtly that he wanted to see Lodge, and the man turned his head to call over his shoulder: "Hey, Lodge, guy here wants to see you!"

The shuffling of feet and the scrape of a chair on boards sounded within. Two men appeared behind the one in the doorway. The taller of them was Lodge. He frowned when he saw

Haney, whom he knew as Blaine the rancher.

"What you want, Blaine?" He shoved the other men aside and stepped out of the dugout.

"I've come for the boy." Haney's voice was quiet, almost toneless.

Lodge shrugged. "Yeh? Ain't seen him. What's the matter? Has he run away?"

Haney's hand dropped to his gun. His voice did not rise, nor did his eyes change. "You can quit stalling," he said. "I've seen Mary. I came for the boy, and I'll take him if I have to drill all three of you."

Lodge laughed. "You better go back and mind your own business, Blaine. You might get hurt. It's three to one." And he gestured toward the two men standing behind him.

"You're mistaken," Haney replied. "It's five to three. I have four men here in the trees, their guns drawn, covering you right now. Kick up a fuss and you're the ones who'll get hurt. I wasn't the only one who saw Mary. Bring out the boy."

"He isn't here, I tell you! I haven't seen him!"

Lodge retorted irritably. "I don't know anything about him. If she told you I did, she was lying to you."

Haney's face whitened. "Step out of the way, you three! I'm coming in and get that boy."

Lodge's eyes narrowed. Not for an instant did he believe that Haney had four men with him, standing there in the trees. The one thought in his drunken treacherous head was that Haney was surely alone, and that they three could fill him with lead before he could make a step.

Lodge went for his gun, and he was not slow. Neither were the two men behind him. Lodge's gun barked the merest flick of time before those of his two companions. But the air was split by the crash of eight guns, instead of three. Malo, Wande, Siletz and Coulone sprang from the trees as the three by the dugout went down. Haney stepped around the fallen bodies and strode into the dugout, Malo and the others close behind him. The room they entered was empty. There was no sign of the boy anywhere.

They overturned everything in which the child, or his body, might be hidden. Still, nothing. Haney suddenly silenced their voices and the sound of their feet upon the floor, by raising his hand in a gesture, bidding them to listen. Then they heard a faint cry, seeming to come from the farther wall of the dugout.

"Mr Blaine! Mr Blaine!"

Haney sprang to the wall, and called back. "Is that you, Danny? Where are you?"

"In the cave," the child's voice answered. "You can shove back that whole wall. Please get me out of here."

"Just sit tight, Danny." Haney flung himself against the plank wall.

In the dark cavern they found the boy, tied into

a chair, black and blue with bruises from the beating Lodge had given him, his eyes swollen and red from crying. Haney cut the filthy strings that tied him, picked him up, and strode out of the dugout holding the child in his arms.

He sent his men back to camp, while he and Malo went to return the boy to Mary. Her relief at seeing him sent her into a flood of tears, and she cried out as Haney placed him in a chair:

"Danny! Did they hurt you?"

Malo saw her snatch a cloth and wipe blood from the boy's cheek. Haney had already turned and hurried out the door. The outlaw was already in the saddle when he overtook him, and Malo mounted his own horse and rode close to the other man's side.

"Haney!" he said sharply. "That boy was not hurt badly, in no place was his skin broken."

"Well?" Haney's voice was quiet and weary.

"There was blood on his cheek. And his cheek was lying against your chest. You were hit?"

"Yes." Haney's head dropped on his breast. "Lodge got me—even as I got him."

As though the last ounce of strength that had upheld him were suddenly departed, Haney slumped in the saddle, limply, his face drained of color.

Again the men sprang up in camp, startled at the approach of Malo and Haney. But this time the horses walked slowly, both men were on

Malo's mount, and Malo held Haney in place on the saddle.

He was not yet unconscious, but he was fast sinking into the shadows from which men do not return. The pallor of death was already upon his face. It held the men dumb as they gathered around him.

"Malo." The pale chilly eyes opened and fastened on Malo's face. "What about Mary, and the ranch? Is there any way?"

"Yes," Malo returned steadily. "All you need do is write out a will. One short line—(I will everything I own to Mary Pike Lodge)—and sign it William Robert Blaine."

The thing was done and the simple will was placed in Malo's pocket. The stony dying eyes closed, only to open again.

"Malo! The reward. My body—to the sheriff. The two thousand—to Mary." Malo nodded, his face expressionless. Haney's hoarse voice sank to a difficult whisper. "Malo—would you—sing that song?"

The stony eyes closed again. Malo lifted his expressionless face. Haney was going out. The throaty tenor rose high and clear.

> "We were wand'ring in the shadows of
>   the pines, my love and I,
> And a wind was blowing softly from the
>   sea—"

A smile come upon Haney's blanched face as he heard.

"You turned away unheeding the tears I could not hide,
You turned away and not a word was said—
On Life's dull pathway the sun no longer shines,
Come, love, and meet me in the shadow of the pines."

Haney was so still that Malo thought he was already gone. Siletz and Coulone turned away their heads. A sob shook Wande. The sound seemed to reach Haney. His eyes opened, glazed and dim, and the stony gaze went beyond Malo, intent and fixed. It was as though he saw someone, someone the others could not see, someone who had come to meet him in the shadow of the pines. His husky voice whispered sharply, one word:

"Margarhita!"

As motionless as the dead man, Malo hunched on his heels, staring, stabbed through by that one word, Margarhita. Slowly and stiffly he got to his feet.

"Damn Margarhita Panzaol!" Wande cursed. "That wife of his was a hellion, Malo. If she finds out he's dead she's liable to come up here and claim the ranch. She wasn't drowned with the boy. She got away and kept going. I saw her afterward. Red never knew. But she's still alive."

"No. I beg your pardon." Malo shook his head slowly. "She is not alive. There *is* justice." And he stumbled away blindly through the sun.

He came back into camp later, his face colorless and stern. "Wande," he said, "have you a pair of scissors?" Wande stared, but he nodded. "Well, get them," Malo requested. "Had Haney any other suit of clothes? Then get them and put them on him."

He stood waiting as the three men removed from Haney's body the blood-stained clothes and put on him clean garments. Then he knelt by the body, and trimmed Haney's long heavy beard to a neat imperial, cut the drooping mustache to a short grizzled brush. The three men stood amazed at the change that had been wrought. The neat beard and mustache changed totally the contour of the white face. From that face the icy finger of death had smoothed familiar lines. The stony eyes were closed. Malo rose to his feet and faced the men.

"I know nothing about Redeye Haney," he said quietly. "But my friend William Robert Blaine was accidentally shot at his ranch this afternoon. He gave me a will leaving everything to Mary Lodge. I am taking his body to the sheriff to prove his death, to make the will valid, and to see that he has decent burial on the hill by his son. I shall not be back."

"But—" Wande floundered for words, "But—that two thousand?"

"I'll see that Mary Lodge gets two thousand dollars," Malo replied.

In less than an hour Pilgrim was saddled and Haney's body lay on a stretcher strapped to the pack saddle on the pack horse. As Malo mounted Pilgrim, a long silence held. Then he pressed Pilgrim with his knees and the two horses started forward. "Goodbye, boys, and good luck."

Three things happened. The sheriff in the nearest town inspected a will, verified a death and helped to make out a deed to Mary Pike Lodge. William Robert Blaine was buried beside his son. And Jason Aaron Orme received this telegram:

TO THIS TOWN PLEASE WIRE ME TWO THOUSAND DOLLARS

JAY.

Chapter XIII

WHO TRAVELS ALONE

The next letter Orme received, he kept. With the letter slipped into his pocket, he went into the house, sat down at his desk and wrote to Malo's father:

My dear brother Gem:

You have asked many times for news of Jay. To my regret I have had so little to give. His letters have been always strikingly brief. But I have just received from him a missive so entirely different from anything he has ever written before that I feel very much stirred about it.

I shall not try to tell you what he says. I take refuge in quoting verbatim sundry paragraphs from his letter. He begins:

"You will see by the postmark on this letter that Pilgrim and I have reached Montana. We have meandered a good three thousand miles. We have grown tough and seasoned. And I am twenty-two. Pilgrim is seven. And it is four years since we left Louisiana."

I had been waiting to hear him say that he had somewhere or other taken up with a chum to share his wanderings. I did not want that, any more than you did. But it was agreed between you and me that I was not to circumscribe him in that respect. So I gave him no direct commands, I merely hinted. Not until now has he ever spoken of it.

"Among other things, you remarked that it was not in the agreement that I should travel alone. You did not even advise it. But you approved of it. I have heeded that more scrupulously than anything else you said. And I have come to sense the secret meaning of the phrase—'He travels fastest who travels alone.' I have come fast and far. I do not mean a mere three thousand miles of distance or a meager four years of time. I have crossed reaches I cannot describe. I have forded currents that swept me under temporarily. But I have come out on shore. Not a sandy shore. Some things I have gained that I must never lose. And some things have gone out of me that I would not have back at any price. I have been freer to choose, freer to go and come, needing to ask no man's opinions on any favored course of action. I have not once deviated from that precept—but I cannot say that I have not been tempted."

He speaks of being tempted *to acquire a comrade, but his action is characteristic of what I would expect in your son. But listen to this:*

"Had it not been for your mildly expressed opinion of the wisdom of keeping to myself, Jason, I should have yielded to temptation on Charley's ranch down in Arizona. It really took determination. The man who so attracted me was one of the punchers there. That man would have made a pal in the most profound sense of the word. His name was Safaro Latizzo. A little Italian. He was all right. He didn't give a damn for anything. But I came over mountains, deserts, valleys and canyons, without him."

Do you see yourself there, Gem? By the time you have finished reading this letter you will wonder whether you are *reading a letter or looking in a mirror. I should like to have seen that Safaro Latizzo. But that is all Jay says concerning him. He doesn't say very much concerning any one person, least of all himself. Yet I believe that his is the most self-revelatory letter I have ever read. A man may be judged also by the things he sees. Note what your son has seen.*

"I have seen strange things in the last four years, Jason. I have seen human beings go to unbelievable lengths. I have seen them commit incredible atrocities and endure beyond understanding. And why? Because of love for someone else. I saw an old man sit silent and bear torture while a bullet was dug from his jawbone, to escape the danger of gangrene. He explained afterward that he simply had to live, because it would crush his wife if anything happened to him. I saw a woman cheat and lie, barter another man's integrity, forget her own soul and degrade her own flesh, because she loved her own man above all other consideration. (But I was a fool, or perhaps merely ignorant. I saw through it too late. They were both hanged.)

"I saw another man take his band and ride upon a nest of vicious scoundrels, kill them and receive his own death wound, to make safe the life of a woman and child. The woman he wished to make safe was the wife of one of the scoundrels. Her child was about the age his own boy would have been had he lived. His own wife had left him, taking the child. The child was drowned, and he thought his wife was also. But she had escaped from the accident. She was the woman who was hanged. And he wanted to make this other woman and child safe for the future in the name of the wife he had lost. He was an outlaw with a price on his head. The last thing he did was to will this woman everything he owned. He requested that his body be turned over to the law, the reward collected, and given to her to keep her and her son from want. (To give his life, and sell his flesh, in the name of a woman—unworthy—whom he had loved and lost.)

"His last wishes were carried out—with a slight variation. He was buried under his own name, beside his son. The notorious outlaw simply disappeared. The woman was taken care of, received the deed to the ranch, and also the money he wanted her to have."

I can vouch for that, Gem. The boy wired me for two thousand dollars. You'll note he doesn't mention it. He never will.

Nor does he mention that it was he who dug the bullet out of that man's jaw bone. But of course it was. I shall quote the rest of his letter without interpolation.

"I have been thinking a great deal. Those people did all those things for love of someone. Love is born, I think, of the gregarious tendency in all humanity; the shrinking from taking any journey alone, since the most terrifying and final one is forced upon us in solitude. Being alone impresses upon a man the realization of the desirability of companionship. Being unloved impresses upon a man the knowledge of what it might mean to have the affection of another human being. Nobody ever loved me, unless my mother did. (There is the possible exception of Lew Sudler.) You never loved me, any more than I loved you. You watched over me and educated me to fulfil an obligation laid upon you by my father. Obligation tends to preclude the spontaneity with which love must issue forth.

"I have respected you, because of your loyalty to my father and mother, and for yourself. I might have loved you. But the blast that stunned you killed all response in you. I came to realize that long ago. So, it followed that I knew little about emotion when I started on this trip. I have accrued some knowledge concerning it. Not much. Merely enough to make me wonder. I don't believe I have missed anything, since I have never known exactly what it was. I have not loved anybody. Only things. Pilgrim, and perhaps the desert, herding cattle under the stars and listening to Saff Latizzo singing, across the herd. But I have learned to hate. To hate, with a hate which shall never lessen and cannot die, three things: any wrong to my integrity, false conceptions, and yellow-haired women."

I said I would not interpolate again. But my thought is too strong for me. I wonder if the woman who was hanged taught him the bitterness of false conception. I wonder if the woman for whom the outlaw died and wanted to sell his flesh had yellow hair. I wonder if he really thinks he is telling the truth when he says he never loved anybody?

See how many he has loved already! The man with the bullet in his jaw, this Latizzo, the outlaw who died, the woman who was hanged, Lew Sudler, his mother, and, I am humble, even me. Lastly—

mostly—he loves you. Though he does not even know that.

Where are you, as you read? The point is this, if you are sitting in your room you will be bareheaded. If you are walking in the yard, you will likely have your hat on. So, if you wear your hat, I ask you to take it off. And read on to the close.

"It's only three years more, isn't it? If I have not loved anyone, I have come to look forward to loving someone. As much as a man can imagine loving a person he has never seen. It is as though I had never seen him. For I can remember only that his curling beard and hair were bright red, and that his name was Gem. I can't explain what it is that has centered my mind upon him. I think perhaps it is because he is my one contact with solidity in a world of mirages. He is my one bond with background, and I have learned what background does for a man. Having seen in others pride in having sprung from noble ancestors, I began to seek the reasons for it. Not alone from the impulse to lay upon another the blame for one's own shortcomings, does a man hark back to the line that bred him. Not alone to bask in the glory of another's achievement, does a man cling to an illustrious line from which he has descended. There is also the intermediate desire to determine by what tendencies heredity has influenced his own course in life; to learn the fatality, the inexorable dominance, of what is in the blood.

"I do not care what circumstances may have brought about this extraordinary situation between him and me. It does not matter where he is, or in what place he hides himself, or for what reason he has chosen to keep me in blank ignorance of all concerning him. In three years I shall see him. And when I do see him, I shall love him. When I hear the explanation of whatever sinister eventualities are to blame for this strange contortion of our lives—I shall remember only that he is my father. I shall remember only that, though for some reason which kept him from being with me and rendered him a vague and mysterious figure, all through my youth—he also remembered that he was my father.

"I do not know why I have written to such length. I just got started and kept going. You needn't feel any obligation to answer. There is so much that you cannot say, and too much that you will not wish to say. I shall understand your silence."

And yet he says he has not loved anybody! He times everything by the day when he shall see you. I think it would not be wise to have him come there. You had best come here, and after he has reached the Iron Kettle I will have him come down and you can meet him here in my house. A fitting place.

There is nothing in his letter to inform you of the name he has taken. I have not had the courage to tell you before. But—it is Malo.

I can feel the shock with which you read it, Gem. That, of all the names in the world from which he might have chosen, he should chance to take Malo! If he should meet Earle Costa somewhere, wearing the name Malo!

I wish he might have had some warning. I wish I could have spoken, just that name. But my tongue was tied. And now it is too late. The whole thing is in more powerful hands than either yours or mine. I will leave you with your thoughts.

Affectionately,

JASON.

Chapter XIV

THE MALO HOMBRE

There ensued, then, three years. And a man moved across the hills of Montana. His face and hands were burned by wind and sun to the color of old walnut. His eyes, red-brown, unreadable and deep, were lit by a nameless and profound glow that all men remarked. His was not a personality that could remain obscure. All men knew him. The bandits in the hills knew him. The sheriffs in the towns knew him. Ranchers knew him. Gamblers knew him. People of every stratum of life knew him. But what he knew he kept to himself.

To all alike he was known by the same title—The Malo Hombre. It was inevitable that he should become a legendary figure. Wherever he went legends preceded him, radiated from him and remained behind him.

Choosing here and there at random a handful of those legends, one attains a perspective of the man behind them. There is, for instance, the legend concerning the outlaw Brig Mertifee.

Mertifee was in the hills. A particularly vicious murder had been committed, and all evidence pointed to Mertifee as the perpetrator of it. The sheriff took a posse and went after Mertifee. And though it was known positively that Mertifee was there, they could not find him. Finally the entire male population of the town attacked the hills—save the Malo Hombre. And the sheriff considered. If the Malo Hombre silently refused to join the hunt for Mertifee, it would be reasoned that he knew where Mertifee was. The sheriff came back to town and confronted the Malo Hombre.

"Malo," he said bluntly, "do you know where Mertifee is?"

Malo brushed an imaginary fleck from the shining butt of his right-hand gun. "Yes," he said, "I do."

"Then why in hell haven't you told me before?" the sheriff demanded in exasperation.

"Nobody can attend to my business quite so efficiently as I can. It's been keeping me busy." And Malo brushed the butt of his other gun.

The sheriff scowled. "We've got to get Mertifee before he leaves his hiding place and skips the country, and the only way we'll get him is by a lead through somebody who knows where he is. No doubt there are half a dozen men in the hills who can locate him, but they're as shy of the law as he is. Even if we could get in touch with them, not one of them would give him up. Crooks hang together. So I'll have to call on you."

"No."

The sheriff stared. “What? You mean you won’t? By God, man, you’ve got to. I command you to, in the name of the law.”

“I recognize but one law,” coldly said the Malo Hombre. “Justice.”

“Justice?” The sheriff snorted with indignation. “Do you dare to stand there and tell me that you don’t consider it justice to bring in the man who murdered Kohl?”

“I don’t think I even intimated any such thing.”

“But you just refused to lead us to Kohl’s murderer!”

“I beg your pardon.” Malo’s voice was frosty. “I declined to lead a half dozen men to surround and slaughter Brig Mertifee, which is quite another thing. You have only circumstantial evidence to point to him as the murderer of Kohl.”

“It may be circumstantial,” the sheriff snapped in irritation, “but Mertifee done it. There’s no doubt of that.”

“Pardon me, but there is doubt of it—so long as your evidence remains solely circumstantial.”

“And is that why you won’t lead us to him?”

“No.” Suddenly the red-brown eyes focussed on the sheriff’s face, and the half-amused voice turned hard. “I know where Mertifee is. He knows that I know it. I have sat in his camp, eaten his bread and meat. I will not take you or any other man where he is to capture him by surprise. But if you will call in every damned man out there running around and accomplishing nothing, I'll go after him myself."

"Alone?" The word was an astonished outcry.

"Alone." Malo's eyes were lit with veiled irony. "By one of those other half-dozen men who know where he is, I will send him word that I am coming. And I will bring him back. If you care to meet me on those grounds, I'll go see my messenger. If not, you're wasting time talking to me."

"Oh, I'll take you up fast enough," the sheriff returned hastily. "I'd be a fool not to. When will you start?"

"As soon as every damn man is back here in this town." The Malo Hombre's eyes glowed with a meaning light. "And it's your job to see that they stay here. Any one that tries to follow me will stop at the first advisable spot I choose, and stay there—permanently." And the Malo Hombre turned on his heel.

But the astonishing part of the affair followed. The Malo Hombre rode into the hills and sought out another outlaw who shared with him the knowledge of Mertifee's hiding place. He sent the outlaw to Mertifee with a terse note:

> Mertifee:
>
> If you killed Kohl you'd better move. I'm coming after you. If you didn't, stay where you are and I'll have dinner with

you when I get there. I give you six hours start.

MALO.

Meanwhile, the sheriff, having called in all men according to Malo's demands, undertook vigilantly to make certain that they stayed in town.

Malo delayed six hours. Then he rode into the hills. He came to Mertifee's hiding place, to find him there. But Mertifee was lying upon his back under a tree, shot through the chest by his own hand. On the ground by his side lay the note Malo had sent, and on it Kohl's diamond ring shot fire upon the scribbled lines.

And then there was the legend of Tommy Patchard. Tommy Patchard was seventy-two years old. He had tramped from California to Alaska, down a tortuous trail of years, seeking gold. All he had ever found was merely enough to secure himself another grubstake for the next venture. He was bent, gnarled, weather-beaten and half blind. But still hope spurred him on.

Many ambitions and dreams had come and gone in Tommy's brain, but only one remained. Tommy lived solely to make a strike big enough to enable him to go to Butte, set himself up in a big hotel and take it easy for the rest of his days. In the little mountain town nearest the canyon where Tommy burrowed into the hillside, the figure of the worn old prospector was a familiar sight. Tommy's hope of ending his days at ease in a hotel in Butte was common property. Men spoke of it jestingly, but with sympathy in their eyes.

It was said that if Tommy had saved all the money he had given away to others in distress, he would now possess more than enough to place him in that Butte hotel for the rest of his days. Which is not an exaggeration. Which explains the sympathy with which men looked at each other when they jested about Tommy Patchard's dream.

Then one day the news broke. Tommy Patchard had made his big strike; in that canyon, in the short tunnel in the hillside, Tommy had found a fabulous vein.

Malo, coming down out of the hills, being fond of old Tommy and delighted at the news of his strike, turned a mile out of his way to make a sociable call and offer his congratulations and found Tommy at the mouth of his tunnel, huddled against the wall, moaning in pain, his faded half-blind eyes blank with despair, his seamed face white and grim with wrath. Malo leaped off his horse and bent over him.

"Tommy—what's happened? What's the matter?"

"Hello, Malo." Tommy managed a wry smile.

"I broke my leg, tryin' to chase the gang that robbed me of my gold. The first time I ever been robbed in my life."

In harsh angry sentences Tommy told. He had mined the last of the vein in the hill. He had the stuff all heaped into one gorgeous pile, ready to take it out. He figured it would bring around twenty thousand dollars. A gang of bandits. It was the Ginsler gang, he knew, who had descended upon him and taken his gold to the last small chunk. Tommy was wilted. He was too old to get over such a blow, to go on any longer. The last flicker of hope was doused. It was the end of the trail.

"Don't you think it." Malo prepared to set the broken leg and bind it. "I'll fix you so you'll be all right and send someone over to stay with you till I get back."

"Where are you going?" Tommy quavered anxiously.

"After your gold," Malo answered, rising and turning toward the spring to fetch water. "I know Ginsler, too."

He made Tommy as comfortable as possible, left water and food close to his hand, and rode away. Crushed in spirit, Tommy watched him out of sight, believing that there was little chance of his ever seeing Malo again. That same evening a broad burly man rode into Tommy's camp, remarking briefly that he had been sent to keep

Tommy company till Malo's return. Another bandit out of the hills, Tommy told himself, and wondered anew at the Malo Hombre's hold on all sorts and conditions of men.

Ginsler looked up with a word of greeting a few hours later as Malo rode into the light of his campfire. "Hello, Malo! Where you bound for?"

"Right here, Ginsler. I came for that gold you took from Tommy Patchard."

Ginsler scowled as Malo got off his horse and stood facing him. The bandit leader got to his feet. "What makes you think you'll get it?" he asked.

"I've no time to waste," Malo answered shortly. "I merely want to see it. I don't believe I want it. Throw it out."

For a moment Ginsler studied him. Then in a curt aside he told his men to bring out a small sack full of the stuff. The man grumbled, but he obeyed. He piled the glittering chunks in a little heap on the ground, and Malo bent to examine them. Then he rose and looked at Ginsler with a short laugh.

"No, Ginsler, I don't want it. I supposed it would be all alike. I just wanted to make sure. That isn't gold, you poor damned fool. It's pyrites."

"What? You ain't stringing me, are you?" Dismay and astonishment were written on the outlaw's face.

"Any time you catch me stringing anybody, kindly let me know," Malo returned. "After all these years, Tommy's big strike is fool's gold. But he doesn't know it, and he never will. And the fact that it proves to be as worthless as so much mud doesn't excuse you, Ginsler. You thought it was gold, too. How much money have you in camp?"

Ginsler stared. "Oh, about four thousand five hundred bucks. What business is it of yours?"

"Well, I'll take the four thousand."

"The hell you will!" Ginsler sneered. "What you going to do with it?"

"I'm taking up a collection for Tommy Patchard. You hombres take your money pretty easily. Tommy Patchard has grubbed for his. Now he's made his big stake, and you fellows rob him of the only worthless stuff he ever owned. In return, he's going to receive at least part of what life owes him. And you're going to contribute your share." His hands lingered suggestively near his guns. "Come on, I'm in a hurry."

Ginsler looked him over curiously. "You really think I'll turn my cash over to you?"

"I know you will," Malo answered. "And I'll turn it over to Tommy. Tell him I took his stuff and got the cash for it. I know several other fellows, gentlemen of your own profession, who will be glad to donate to Tommy's old age fund. Go on, Ginsler, get it!"

Suddenly Ginsler laughed aloud. "Damned if I don't! Leave the guns alone, Malo. Yeh, I'll donate. But I wouldn't do it for any other damn man that packs a gun. Pete, bring out our cash."

Malo rode away from Ginsler's camp toward another. For fifteen days he rode, and collected eleven thousand dollars. He went then to another town, and for the second time he wired to Orme. This time he asked for four thousand dollars. The next morning, with fifteen thousand dollars stuffed inside his shirt, he started for Tommy's tunnel.

He told Tommy he had turned over the ore and got the cash, to save him the trouble, since he had a game leg, but it had only brought fifteen thousand. He left Tommy Patchard in a Butte hotel lobby, his mending leg on a stool, sunk in the depths of an easy chair. Tommy's money was safe in the bank. Around Tommy was gathered a group of admiring newfound friends. As Malo turned away, Tommy asked if he would not accept a reward.

The Malo Hombre stood for a moment and filled his eyes. He saw a weathered face beaming with delight. He saw a worn old body sunk luxuriously into a padded chair. He saw faded eyes, eyes so near blind that they had not known fool's gold from the real, gleaming excitedly over the prospect of the future. He saw thin old lips quiver with emotion as a broken old voice told complacently for the tenth time of the long hard life that had led to the big strike.

"No thanks, Tommy," said the Malo Hombre. "I've had my reward."

The legends spread through the hills, across the plains and down the valleys of Montana. To mention the Malo Hombre was to bring to men's minds a figure as familiar as the Rocky Mountains.

Lew Sudler heard his men on the Iron Kettle speak of the Malo Hombre. And he smiled, and wondered who the man was, and had a passing curiosity to see him.

Adjacent to the Iron Kettle, the Cross Eight ranch had failed and been abandoned years ago. Lately, it had been purchased by a cattle man from another state, Dolf Kubik. Kubik had heard of the Malo Hombre. He stood in the barn, smiling to himself as his foreman, Wedge Crossby, talked with the boys of the legendary figure. Kubik walked out of the barn and along the fence, his head bent, musing, glad that through young blood the old West still lived.

He paused as he heard horses coming down the lane, and glanced up to see a stranger upon a big brown animal. "Evenin', Stranger," he greeted.

"Good evening." The walnut brown face of the stranger wrinkled into a smile and red-brown eyes glowed down at Kubik. "Have you room to put a man up over night?"

"Yes, sure," Kubik returned heartily. "Put your horses up in the barn and come in and eat with the boys. My name's Kubik. And this," he paused as a tall man with lank grey hair and a square face, came toward him, "This is my foreman, Wedge Crossby."

The stranger swung off his horse and acknowledged the introduction. "Pleased to meet you, Crossby. My name's Malo."

Crossby darted a glance at Kubik. Kubik started. "Say," Kubik exclaimed excitedly, "are you the man they call the Malo Hombre?"

"Never heard of him," Malo grinned. "Who's he?"

Inside of half an hour the Cross Eight boys, behind his back, were boasting to each other that the Malo Hombre had stopped to stay all night at their ranch. The Malo Hombre stood out by the corrals and gazed across the hills. Just over those bluffs and stretches of sage brush not many miles beyond, lay the Iron Kettle.

Chapter XV
WINDBREAK

Morning came. Breakfast was eaten. Malo went to the barn to get Pilgrim and the pack horse ready to go on to the Iron Kettle. Before he reached the stall where Pilgrim had spent the night, he heard his name called hesitatingly. Malo turned to face Dolf Kubik.

Kubik's very blue eyes were anxious. "I wanted to ask you if you couldn't stay here for a little while. I'm kind of in a little jackpot and I need somebody to help me out. You're the first man I've seen that was just made to fit the job. Couldn't you stay?"

Malo studied for a moment, his penetrating glance passing lightly over Kubik's distressed face. "Why yes, I could stay on anywhere from a week to a month, if I can be of any service to you. My destination isn't far, and another month in reaching it won't make a great deal of difference to me."

"Well, it'll make a world of difference to me. Just wait a minute." Kubik turned and hurried out of the barn.

Malo leaned against the corner of Pilgrim's stall, waiting and thinking. Dolf Kubik, with his big fat round jolly face, habitually on the verge of smiling, revealed himself so blatantly that his character was manifest in spite of his efforts to hide behind a blustering geniality. The perspicacious could discern with little effort that that genial front was a fictitious facade of the spirit, maintained for the purpose of concealing an unconquerable shyness.

A little later Kubik came out of the ranch house and requested Malo to ride out on the range with him. Malo saddled Pilgrim and joined him. The two men rode out to a range where a group of saddle horses were feeding. They cut out a small bunch of the horses and drove them back to the ranch.

When the animals were safely inside the horse pasture, Kubik got off his horse, walked up to the fence and beckoned Malo to join him. "You see that sorrel over there?" Kubik hesitated, shot a glance at Malo, then went on quickly. "Nobody has ever tried to ride him. I never would let anyone touch him. Not that he's mean. I just didn't want him spoiled. He's of fine stock and I want him broke right." He stopped again, ran a finger around the inside of his loose shirt collar, swallowed and made another start. "I have heard you're a great hand with hosses. I wanted you to look the sorrel over and tell me if you think he'd make a suitable hoss for—for—" Kubik averted his eyes. His voice seemed to have stuck in his throat. His round face flushed a painful pink, to the very roots of his blond hair. "For a—for a lady!" he blurted. He gulped, yanked a bandana handkerchief from his pocket and mopped the perspiration from his face.

Malo leaned on the fence and looked the sorrel gelding over with a professional and critical eye. The horse would make an ideal mount for a woman.

Kubik was eager to have the sorrel broken soon, and Malo was anxious to go on to the Iron Kettle. Malo brought the animal up the next day, and put him in the corral by the barn. Wedge Crossby came out of the barn and approached him.

"I see Dolf hasn't lost any time." Crossby nodded at the sorrel. "I knew the minute Dolf began to study you at the table last night that he was going to ask you to break the horse." Crossby stepped closer and leaned an arm upon the corral fence. "The lady is to have the privilege of naming the horse herself."

"What's the matter, Crossby? Is there some mystery about the sorrel and the lady?"

"No." Crossby shook his head. "There's no mystery, but there is a story. That's why I come out here to talk to you. I want you to understand. Poor old Dolf. I am darned sorry for him. I'm afraid it ain't no use. I never would have believed that Dolf would fall for a woman, till this one come along. Then he sure fell hard. We was then down on his ranch in Wyoming, the D Bar K. A fella named Calleot bought the ranch next to the D Bar K a few years ago, and he and Dolf was good friends right from the start. Three years ago Calleot's sister Ellen come down to visit him.

"Well, while she was at Calleot's ranch she wanted to get herself a saddle horse. Had her heart set on a sorrel with a cream-colored mane and tail. Calleot didn't have none, but he seen this colt on Dolf's range. So he brought Miss Ellen over to the D Bar K to see if she liked the horse and would Dolf sell him. The minute Dolf seen her it was all up with him. She could have had any horse on his ranch.

"The sorrel was sure enough just what she fancied, and Dolf told her she could sure have him, as soon as he was old enough to get broke proper. She went home, then, and Dolf was like a lost dog, until he thought of writin' to her on the excuse of telling her how the colt was getting along. That colt sure got awful important, the way Dolf had to write about him.

"But Dolf didn't like the idea of being so far away from her. She'd been living here in Montana for years. The more he thought about it, the worse it got. So he sent me up here to buy a ranch near to Miss Calleot. The Cross Eight was the only thing I could hook, and I got it for almost nothing. He come up, stocked the ranch and hired a flock of punchers and settled in Montana just to be near Ellen Calleot. Ever since then, he's been on the lookout for a man to break the sorrel for her."

Crossby hesitated. "It's kind of hard to explain the rest of it, but I reckon you'll understand. Dolf don't only want you to break the horse, he wants you to take it to Miss Ellen, too. He wants to give her the horse, and he ain't got the face to take it to her himself, and to tell her he moved up here just to be near her."

"You mean he's been here nearly a year and she doesn't know it yet?"

Crossby nodded. "Yeh. Why, you know what he does? He writes to her and sends the letter down to the D Bar K and has the boys mail it to her from there. And the boys forward her answers up here. He's awful bashful. But that ain't all. Dolf's a rough old codger, ain't up to all the fine ways like she is. He wanted some man to speak to her for him, some man that could talk good. Minute I heard you talkin' at the table last night and seen Dolf listening to you so close, I knowed what was on his mind. You understand me, don't you?"

"I think I do. Quite clearly." Malo did not smile. "And he wants me to come back and report faithfully how Miss Ellen received the horse, his gift that is meant to show her his intentions toward her."

"That's it. You can tell if she acts like she was

pleased, or if she don't want nothing to do with him. By God, Malo, I hope she don't turn him down! I reckon I ain't got no more to say."

Breaking the sorrel proved as simple a task as Malo had thought it would. He rode the horse off and on, and worked him for nearly a month, then set off from the Cross Eight, riding Pilgrim and leading the sorrel. Miss Calleot's home lay forty-five miles from the Cross Eight, in the opposite direction from the Iron Kettle, ninety miles from Lew. Malo told himself grimly that he hoped Ellen Calleot would prove worthy. (Women were not, sometimes. He thought of William Blaine.) And he hoped that Ellen Calleot might not prove to have yellow hair.

It was nearing evening when he arrived at her home. He had traveled slowly, taking pains that the horse should arrive fresh and the journey for that reason had occupied about twice as much time as was really necessary. Now, in sight of his destination, he gazed at it in surprise. A rambling log bungalow it was, set on top of a low bluff, almost hidden from sight by clambering vines in a grove of pine trees. Malo followed the winding road to the top of the bluff.

An old gardener was at work raking mown grass from the smooth surface of a spreading lawn. Malo rode in through the open gates and the old gardener came toward him with a greeting, squinted nearsighted eyes at Malo, at

Pilgrim, and lastly at the sorrel. His gaze riveted on the white-maned animal, and he moved closer. "Say, that's the hoss Miss Ellen bought down in Wyoming, ain't it? She was tellin' me about him. Said she was to get him sometime this summer. That's him, ain't it?"

"Yes." Malo nodded. "Would you mind telling her that he has arrived."

But the errand was unnecessary. Ellen Calleot had seen Malo ride in, had recognized the horse, and was coming down the steps of the house.

Malo scrutinized her from under his hat brim as she drew near. Her face was unlined and smooth. The fine brown hair glinting in the evening sun showed no trace of grey. But in her deep-set eyes, as she paused and looked up at him, he saw an indefinable sadness that was reflected in the droop of her mouth.

"Did Mr Kubik send you all the way up here from Wyoming on horseback?"

"No, ma'am." Malo shook his head. "Mr Kubik isn't there any more. He has moved to Montana. He now owns the Cross Eight. I brought the horse only that far, after breakfast this morning. I broke him in on the Cross Eight."

"Oh! Mr Kubik is in Montana?" She glanced again at the sorrel. "Jim, put the horses up in the barn." She did not speak again until the gardener had taken the horses and started toward the barn. Then she lifted her gaze to Malo. "If you will get down and kindly come into the house, I will give you a check for the horse."

He thanked her as he swung out of the saddle, and joined her as she started toward the house.

"Since you broke him in, I should like to ask you if he has any particular tricks for which I need to watch, Mr—I don't know your name?"

"My name is Malo. No, there's nothing to watch for in him. He's a good horse."

She stopped abruptly as they started to ascend the steps. "You say your name's Malo? Why—you aren't the Malo Hombre?"

"Who's he?" And Malo grinned.

A brilliant smile curved her mouth. "Why, how delightful! To know that my horse was broken and brought to me by so famous a person as the Malo Hombre! Really, you must stay to dinner. I won't take no for an answer. You won't refuse me that courtesy, surely."

"Well, no, I don't see how I can—if you put it that way," Malo answered.

She led him into the house, took his hat, hung it on an old walnut hall tree and led him into the living room. Malo seated himself in a deep chair, wondering inwardly about that look of sadness in her deep eyes.

"Now, won't you tell me more about the horse?" She took a chair a few feet away, facing him. "I shall call him Shadow. No matter why. I should judge you had no trouble breaking him."

"None at all. He broke as easily as any horse I ever worked." Malo ceased speaking abruptly, his gaze riveted on the far side of the room. "Pardon me for changing the subject so suddenly. But I couldn't help noticing that excellent painting."

Her gaze turned to the canvas that occupied most of the far end wall. It had been done with a master touch; a high leaning windbreak of eucalyptus trees. Beyond the windbreak lay a sun-washed sandy beach. Beyond the beach the long roll of white-capped waves broke beneath a blue white sky. Malo had the sense of scenting the pungent perfume of the eucalypti, of feeling in his face the breeze blowing in off the sea.

He leaned forward in his chair. "It's one of the finest things I ever saw. It's alive. You can fairly *smell* those trees."

Ellen Calleot laughed softly. "Yes, you can. That isn't your imagination." She leaned to the window, drew back the curtain and disclosed on the sill a small bottle of colorless liquid. "Eucalyptus oil. I smudge the lower edge of the frame with it frequently. I love the odor."

"I see. But I believe I should have smelled them without that. How did you ever get so huge a canvas up here?"

"It was taken out of the frame and wrapped over a padded pole. It is called Windbreak. It was—" The voice of the house-maid, calling her, interrupted. She rose hurriedly, and Malo had a swift conviction that she was glad of an excuse to discard the subject of the painting. “Excuse me for a moment. Just make yourself at home. Perhaps you play. If so, there is an organ. I will return shortly.”

Malo’s eyes followed her till the closing door hid her from sight, then came back to the great painting. He sat lost in contemplation of its excellent execution, its intense appeal. He rose and walked a few steps toward it, then stepped over by the organ and looked at the canvas from that angle. It was the same from any point of view. It dominated the room.

He rested an arm on the top of the organ, and felt a sharp-edged object under his elbow. A mouth harp was lying on top of the organ, the end of it projecting from under his arm. He picked up the little harp. He fingered it, raised it to his lips and blew on it absent-mindedly, his eyes again raised to the painting.

Some incongruous association between eucalypti and pine trees brought William Blaine to his mind. He fancied he saw the wind swaying the tops of that windbreak, heard it soughing very like the sound in the pines that Blaine had loved. He visioned the dying outlaw lying by the campfire. He was so deeply engrossed with that inner scene that he was not aware Ellen Calleot had entered the room until he heard her cry out sharply:

"Oh, why do you play *that?* Don't! Please don't!"

The melody stopped short. Malo turned to face her, brought back abruptly to his surroundings. Her features were quite white. The sadness in her eyes was deepened. She came toward him swiftly as he laid the mouth harp back on the organ.

"That's Jim's mouth harp. He leaves it lying about everywhere. I hope you won't think me brusque, Mr Malo, but I can't endure that song. How did you ever come to play it?"

"It was the result of a train of thought evoked by your picture."

Her eyes were almost hard from her effort to maintain her threatened composure. "I was taken so unaware, hearing you play that particular melody. And you don't know *how* you were playing it. It has memories for you—too?"

"It has."

"I'm sorry. Dinner is ready, please."

When they went back into the living room, Malo was wondering if he hadn't better bring into the conversation the mission on which he had come. She spoke suddenly, with a thin edge of desperation in her tone.

"I think I owe you an explanation, Mr Malo. You liked Windbreak. I painted it."

"You did?" Malo sat up in his chair, his gaze going from the painting to her. "Then you're an artist, Miss Calleot!"

"No, I beg your pardon. I'm not. I used to

believe, long ago, that I might someday become an artist. I was very young then, as you are now. I was to have been married. The man wanted me to be content with a home and paint there merely for my amusement. I couldn't see it that way. I wanted a career. We quarreled over it, foolishly and hotly, there by the windbreak. Each of us vowed the other must give in and neither ever yielded. After it was too late, I found how vain and foolish I had been. I wasn't an artist after all. I painted Windbreak because my heart was in it; another of like excellence is beyond my capacity. I can bear to look at it and remember him, but I can't bear to hear the song he loved. The song I was singing when we quarreled. You—quarreled with someone, too?"

"No." Malo shook his head slowly, but he did not look at her. "It was another man who quarreled with someone. I sang it for him as he died."

"Who—*who* died?" Her face was ghastly as she leaned toward him, her hands gripped together.

"Not the man you mean. It was his wife, and she died before he did."

"Oh." She leaned back in her chair, limply, and her hands dropped apart. "I didn't think it could have been he. No doubt he has forgotten it long since. But I—forget poorly."

Malo sat silently looking up at the great painting, and there came into his ears a line of the song: "And a shadow came between my love and me." Ellen Calleot had named the sorrel Shadow. He heard her voice.

"He was going to give me a sorrel horse with a cream-colored mane and tail. For a long time I couldn't bear the thought of the horse. Then I wanted it. But I had a hard time finding one."

Malo said nothing. The silence lengthened until it became unendurable. He got to his feet.

"I must be going, Miss Calleot. There is something I want to tell you before I leave. Not about what you have said. There are times when silence gives better proof of understanding than speech."

"I don't want you to go." Ellen Calleot rose and stretched out a detaining hand. "Jim sleeps on the ground floor and there's a guest room on the ground floor also. Won't you stay over and go back in the morning after breakfast? Won't you stay and help me to become gay and casual again?"

"Again, what can I say when you put it like that?" And Malo resumed his chair.

It was the better part of two hours later when she finally showed him across the hall into the guest room. When the door had closed between them and he was alone with his thoughts, he rolled a cigaret, lit it and paced across the room, anathematizing himself.

"A fine emissary you are! A hell of an emissary. But hang it, what can a fellow say to a woman who paints a picture that is a masterpiece and lives with it because it keeps before her the spot where she used to walk with a man she can't forget? Whose composure breaks at the sound of his favorite song? Who looks all over the country to find a horse like the one he was going to give her? It would take a damned smart emissary to figure that out!"

He turned his back upon himself in disgust, remembering Dolf Kubik's eager face. Ellen Calleot had named the horse Shadow. It was fitting. She lived in shadow. He stopped short, turned and started toward the door. It had come to him what he could say.

She sat just beyond the organ, her hands folded in her lap, her eyes on the painting, and there seemed to drift around her the pungent odor of the eucalypti. She saw him, from the oblique angle of her gaze, but neither her body nor her eyes moved. Malo spoke.

"There is no price upon Shadow, Miss Calleot. Dolf wanted me to tell you that the horse is a gift, a small token of his high regard for you. To live in shadow is to die alive. Dolf Kubik, if you can see him clearly, is all sunlight. You can't, nobody can, bring shadow to light. But you can let the sunshine in. Will you try to consider that? To give Dolf hope?"

Without removing her eyes from the painting she nodded slowly, once. "I had suspected that. His feeling for me, I mean. Yes, I'll try."

Chapter XVI

RETURN

All the way back to the Cross Eight in the morning, Malo thought of Ellen Calleot and the man she could not forget. A half mile distant from the ranch buildings, he sighted Crossby riding at a jog pace along the trail toward him. The moment he came within speaking distance, the foreman greeted him.

"I've been on the lookout for you. I wanted to see you before Dolf did. Which way does the wind blow?"

Malo countered: "Do you know any man around here who used to be engaged to her years ago?"

"I know quite a bit about it, though I don't know the man's name, but Dolf don't know nothing about it. She used to live in California. That's where she and this fellow kept company together. They split up over some fool thing."

"Yes. Just that," Malo agreed. "A fool thing."

"I reckon he's forgot all about it by this time. You saw her gardener, maybe? He's my uncle, Jim Crossby. Him and her gets along. She talks to him sometimes, and he talks to me, and I add up five and five. Dolf ain't got much chance if she won't stop thinking of that other fella. That fella stands between Dolf and Ellen like a ghost."

"Maybe, Wedge. But some ghosts can be laid. We'd better change the subject, Wedge. There's Dolf, waiting for us."

The two men rode into the lane, to see Kubik leaning upon the fence and watching their approach eagerly. Crossby passed on without remark. But Malo drew rein opposite the boss and smiled down at him.

"I intended coming back last night, Dolf. But we got to talking and she asked me to stay till this morning. I told her you were giving her the sorrel, and hinted that you'd like her to take you along with him. She named him Shadow. I suggested to her that you were a pretty good scout to have around—permanently. She agreed to think about it."

"Did she now?" Kubik stammered, flushed. He turned and fled precipitately.

Malo rode on to the barn, his face sober, his red-brown eyes deep. He knew he had not seen the last of Ellen Calleot. The next morning Malo saddled Pilgrim, took his pack horse, and started on the last lap for the Iron Kettle.

The noon sun shone down upon the Iron Kettle. A man, riding a big brown horse and leading a pack horse, halted his animals at the top of a slope overlooking the ranch buildings from the north. Over his head three tall pine trees rose, shading a great stone on which was chiseled a terse epitaph: *Mrs Leddby Died And At Rest.* He removed his hat, bent his head and sat motionless in the saddle contemplating the gigantic rock. Twenty years ago they had come there, to remain under the protection of Lew until she died. For nearly sixteen years that great stone had lain above her. He raised his head at last, and looked down at the ranch house.

Lew Sudler was that near. He did not glance at the stone again. But he rode down the slope carrying his hat in his hand, and did not replace it until he had passed out of sight of his mother's grave. The Iron Kettle looked exactly as it had looked when he left it. No one was in sight. He dismounted by the barn, and as he did so a man stepped out of the bunkhouse and walked swiftly toward him.

Malo's eyes narrowed at sight of him. The man was heavily built, uncouth and repellant. His flat nose added bestiality to a face rendered crude in the making. Little greenish eyes looked out from beetling brows.

"What'll you have?" he growled surlily.

"I want to see Lew Sudler," Malo answered, tensed, antagonistic, on the defensive.

A peculiar dry grin crossed the man's sullen face. "This place is gettin' right popular lately. We got more company than we know what to do with. But go on in. One more won't make things any worse, I guess." He turned and went back into the bunkhouse.

Malo stood looking after him. Something was wrong. The presence of such a man on the Iron Kettle was in itself a warning that things were not as they should be. Malo put his horses in the barn and started briskly toward the house. Unconsciously, he felt for his guns, ascended the steps and rapped upon the back door. There was no reply. He rapped again. A light step came from within, and the door opened to disclose a woman.

She was young, with a fine pale face, and grey eyes that looked out at him from an aura of shining yellow hair. The fact that her grey eyes were large with fright did not soften Malo's swift anger. She had yellow hair. A yellow-haired woman in Lew's house! His face turned grim, expressionless, cold.

"I'd like to see Lew," he said shortly. "Is he at home?"

"Why, yes—" The woman hesitated. "He's here. You could see him, if it's important. But he can't talk to you. He—he's sick. Is there anything I could tell him?"

"No. I prefer to see him personally." Malo pushed the door wider, deliberately stepped by her and entered the room.

It was the kitchen. He needed no one to tell him where to find Lew. He remembered where Lew's bedroom opened off the kitchen. The door was closed. He walked swiftly toward it, conscious that the woman had closed the outer door and was following him. Ignoring her, impatient at her presence, he turned the knob and swung open the door leading into Lew's room.

In that first moment, Lew was all he saw. And he saw him with a feeling of shock that slowed his footsteps. Sudler was lying upon his bed, flat on his back, motionless with a peculiar flaccidity. His eyes, staring from a drawn, colorless face, had turned to the door. As Malo entered, Sudler's gaze centered on him, puzzled and inquiring. Malo paused at his bedside, and Sudler's eyes held his, unwinking.

The puzzlement in Sudler's gaze increased. This man was a stranger. Yet there was something about him which was not strange. The red-brown eyes, lit with a peculiar glow, were familiar. Sudden recognition vanquished the puzzled inquiry. Sudler tried to smile, and achieved a wry grimace. He had said he would know it again anywhere this side of hell. Those were the eyes of the boy who had run away sixteen years ago. In this brown-faced man towering over him, the boy had come back.

Malo saw the recognition in his eyes. He sat down on the edge of the bed and laid a hand over Sudler's still fingers. "You know me, don't you, Lew? It's Jay. I've been coming back to you for seven years. For the Lord's sake, Lew, what's happened to you?"

"He's been struck on the head," answered a voice across the room.

For the first time Malo gave his attention to the two men who sat beyond the bed. He raised his gaze to them, scrutinizing them intently. The man who had spoken was a slight man, under medium height, with thick smooth brown hair, a close-cropped grey beard and mustache and queerly expressionless hazel eyes. The man went on speaking quietly:

"The blow caused a hemorrhage in the medulla. The pressure of the blood has resulted in temporary paralysis, which will endure until the blood clot is absorbed. He will be able to move and talk in a few days, less than a week I think. But complete recovery will take a long time."

"You're a doctor?"

"Of sorts," the man answered dryly. "I would take it that you must be an old friend of Mr Sudler?"

"I certainly am. I've known him ever since I was a child. How was he hurt?"

"We have been unable to learn." The man gestured to the bigger man who sat just beyond him. "Mr Taight, here, is also an old friend of Mr Sudler. Mr Taight and Miss Taight came west on a tour for Mr Taight's health. I came along as physician. Mr Taight stopped to see Mr Sudler.

We found him like this. So I took him on, also, and now have two patients instead of one. My name is Costa."

Malo felt himself go rigid. His eyes chilled. His brain clicked open upon a picture, like a camera shutter; upon a picture of Mammy Cindy standing by the stone pillars in Jason's driveway. He heard her voice echoing in his ears; "Guido Costa, honey. He's got a brother. Ah sees trouble."

It was not a common name. There was every chance that this man might be Guido Costa's brother, the man of whom Cindy had warned him. If he was, there was an old score of some kind to be settled, a score of which Costa knew, and of which he did not. But Costa could find no significance in the name Malo. He said shortly:

"Thanks. My name's Malo."

He turned his gaze back to Sudler. By so doing he missed the sudden glare that flickered into Earle Costa's expressionless eyes. Seemingly as relaxed and indolent as was his habitual attitude, Costa tensed. After twenty years—Malo! Not by any expression of his face, or by the least move of his body, did the detective evidence any trace of the sudden wild agitation that boiled within him. But his gaze, brooding on Malo, was as the gaze of a panther ready to leap.

Malo raised his eyes to Taight. His passing glance fell upon the yellow-haired woman.

Anger stirred him. Cindy's words flashed into

his mind again. He drove them off impatiently. Hadn't he loved one woman with yellow hair, and hated her, and turned her over to the law? Wasn't that enough? What a farce of a homecoming. Lew stricken with paralysis. A yellow-haired woman in the house. And Costa sitting by Lew's bed. And Lew paralyzed because he had been struck on the head.

"Mr Taight?" Malo asked. "Was it accident? Did he fall or something of the kind?"

Taight shifted in his chair, uneasy and concerned. "You must remember that we found him like that. Of course we questioned the men. They didn't know anything about it. They were very uncivil. Things are in a bad way around here. I tell you frankly I don't like his men at all."

Sudler made a faint harsh noise with his throat. Malo turned a quick gaze upon him, and Taight sprang up from his chair to the other side of the bed. Sudler was making a desperate attempt to speak. A guttural rasp that died away was all the sound he could achieve.

"Don't try to talk, Lew." Malo leaned close. "I can guess what you want to say. That these fellows here are not your men."

"How did you know?" Costa inquired, quickly.

"I saw one of them outside," Malo answered. "And if the rest of them are anything like him, they certainly don't belong on this ranch. How many of them are there?"

"I've seen five," Costa said.

"Well, one thing is sure." Malo rose to his feet. "We've got to get some information, someway. I'm going out and talk to that fellow I saw. Maybe I can persuade him to start a little conversation."

"Just a minute, Mr Malo." Bruce Taight straightened, and stepped around the foot of the bed. "I think I know you, now. You're the boy Lew took to raise, and who disappeared from the Iron Kettle, aren't you? I'd like to ask you something else. I've been interested in what I've been hearing about a fellow they called the Malo Hombre. I'd like to ask—are you he?"

"Yes."

Taight smiled grimly. "Well, that knocks one of my theories into a hat. Earle, that's Mr Costa, told you the story we trumped up to tell when we arrived. There's nothing the matter with me, nor is there with Cynara—Miss Taight. Earle is a physician, yes. But he's a better detective. We came knowing Lew was in trouble.

"I live in New York. I had been on a trip to Florida. I came home to find a queer communication from Lew. In it he told me he was at the point of death, that the ranch was saddled with mystery, and that some damned ugly outfit was riding herd on him. I couldn't decipher the message myself, called Earle in. He decoded it in about ten minutes. So I hit for the West, and Earle insisted on coming along. You know what we found when we got here. None of us had any idea these men were not Lew's regular employees. Why, hell! These fellows must be the damned ugly outfit he meant!"

Taight whirled, bent over Sudler and inquired excitedly: "Is that it? Are they the fellows you meant?"

Sudler only gazed at them, his eyes blank with astonishment.

"He doesn't know what you mean," Malo put in quickly, joining Taight at the bedside. Lew only gazed upward steadily. But the live eyes in the paralyzed body managed to send a message. Clearly he did not in the least know what Taight meant.

"What's the matter, Lew? What in hell's coming off here, anyhow?" Taight swore violently, and he saw Malo's eyes flick a glance at Cynara. "Oh, don't mind Cynara," Taight said shortly. "If I didn't cuss she'd think I was sick. Lew, where the hell are your men? Can't you try to make some sign?"

"Don't irritate him, Bruce," Costa put in quickly. "We've annoyed him too much already. We'll have to put our heads together and see what we can determine without his aid. It looks as though Malo would be of material aid. He knows this country, and I've never seen it before. What do you suspicion, Malo?"

"A number of things," Malo answered dryly.

"You said you tried to question these fellows. Did you get no information at all?"

Costa smiled enigmatically. "The big fellow with the flat nose said he was the foreman. He said Sudler was sick with a fever. Mr Sudler had a slight fever, all right. But the minute I examined him I knew what was wrong."

"Well, we're going to find out a few things pronto, Dr Costa." Malo took the chair at the head of the bed and leaned close to Sudler. "Lew, I want to ask you a few questions. If your answer is yes, merely close your eyes. To give us a negative answer, keep them open. Were your men driven away?" Sudler's eyes held his unwinking. "Did they go voluntarily?" Still the negative sign answered him. "They didn't quit? There was no fight? Were you hurt before they went? No? Afterward, eh?" That time Sudler's eyes closed in confirmation. "Do you know who struck you?" Again the affirmative sign.

"Let's see. Your crew disappeared after you were hurt. You were knocked out, and when you came to you found these crooks here. Is that right?" Sudler's eyes closed. "Do you know how many of these fellows are here? No? How many have you seen?" Malo counted to five before Sudler's eyes closed again. "You've seen five, too, eh? Have you any idea who they are or where they come from?" Sudler's eyes remained open.

Costa spoke suddenly. "Mr Malo, you have already proved the value of being familiar with the country and its ways. You have proved the value of knowing just what questions to ask. Regardless of anything else, we're compelled to combine our efforts to solve this thing."

"I should suppose that would be taken for granted." Malo looked him straight in the face. What did Costa mean by that *regardless of anything else?* Why did he use the word *compelled?*

"Doubtless." Something dangerous sparked unseen in Costa's eyes. "I wonder if you know any of the other ranchers in the neighborhood who might be able to give us a line on these fellows here?"

"I don't know anyone else around here at all. But I might get in touch with some of them, anyway." And Malo thought of Ridelle. The Floating R was the nearest ranch. Even though Ridelle had picked a quarrel with Sudler, or so he had heard, that was of little moment now. Any rancher would drop petty personal differences to aid another rancher in distress. Again Malo questioned Sudler. "Lew, how about Kurt Ridelle? Think it would be of any use to get him over here?" To his surprise a malignant gleam came into Sudler's eyes, a gleam of anger and protest. Very evidently Lew Sudler did not want Kurt Ridelle around the Iron Kettle. Malo turned to

Taight. "You said the message you got from Lew was queer. In what way?"

"It was concealed in a hymn book," Taight answered. "Pricked into the page with a pin. And I never knew Lew to have any interest in hymn books."

Malo heard a hoarse rasping sound from the bed. He turned his head quickly. Sudler was straining to bring words to his flaccid throat. "What is it, Lew?" Malo asked. "You wanted to say something about the message you sent Mr Taight?" Sudler's eyes closed. "You knew something pretty bad was afoot when you sent it, of course?" Sudler's eyes remained open. "You mean you weren't expecting trouble? Then, why did you send that message to Taight?" Still Sudler's eyes remained open, focused on Malo's, strained and tense, desperately striving to communicate something.

"Maybe he means he didn't send it," Costa put in, watching Sudler intently.

Sudler's eyes closed with a swift vehemence.

Malo bent closer to the injured rancher. "Is that what you're trying to tell us? That you did not send the hymn book?" Sudler's eyes fairly snapped shut.

"Well I'll be damned!" Taight stared as though he thought Sudler crazed. "Then where in God's name did it come from?"

"Queer business." Costa rose and strolled

over to the bed. "Taight gets a message from Montana, marked with the brand of the Iron Kettle, outlining a dire situation and calling for help. It is signed with Sudler's initials. We race across the continent in answer to the call. We find Sudler on the floor, paralyzed from a blow on his head. His crew has disappeared and a rough lot of gangsters are in possession of the ranch. Sudler denies sending any message, and does not know anything about one being sent. Taight *said* it wasn't his writing. The whole country must be cuckoo!"

Suddenly Malo became aware that Cynara Taight, still huddled in her chair, was looking at him with increased apprehension in her eyes.

He got to his feet, and stood looking down at Sudler. "The first thing I'm going to do is see what you have in the kitchen, Lew. I'm hungry."

"I'd be glad to get you something." Cynara rose and came to the foot of the bed, making her offer with nervous eagerness.

Malo glanced at her coldly. She had offered to get him something to eat merely because she was frantic for something to do. To suffer the service would be a kindness to her. Malo said shortly;

"Thank you. But don't go to any trouble. Anything will do."

As he followed her to the kitchen, he was

reminded unpleasantly of another yellow-haired woman who had fed him—and betrayed him to himself. He said to himself; "Damn Cindy and her yellow-haired women."

Chapter XVII

AN ALLY OF JUSTICE

By the stockade on the Floating R ranch, two men sat and leaned against the fence. They were laughing loudly. The elder of the two was a man in his late forties. His darkly tanned features were squared and strong, and sharp blue eyes marked a contrast with his sunburned skin. His hat lay on his knee, and the sun fell upon his short brush of drab brown hair. He bore the name of George Eckhart.

The younger man was a small dark-faced Italian. His face was eloquent of his emotional nature. He bore the name of Safaro Latizzo. It was Latizzo who finally checked his diminishing chuckles and spoke:

"Poor old Articulo. Sure was a job we put up on him, wasn't it?"

"Where did you first meet up with him?" Eckhart asked.

"Down at Charley's ranch in Arizona, where you and me got together." Latizzo answered. "I already told you that. He left there just a little while before you come. He didn't like cow nursing much."

"What made you go to Arizona in the first place?" Eckhart probed. "You told me once you used to live up here in Montana when you was a kid."

"Sure I did." Latizzo agreed. "I was born right here on the Floating R. My father was one of Kurt's first crew of men. Dad died here; Mother died here too. I stayed on with Kurt. Didn't have no folks anywhere else. But after a few years I got curious to see something of the rest of the world. There was a big free-for-all rodeo down in Arizona, so I thought I'd go down there, and see the country. I liked the place, got a job on Charley's ranch and stayed."

But Eckhart was not to be evaded. "And that's where you met this Articulo fellow, Saff?"

"Yes." Latizzo frowned. "He went back to New York to some of his relatives. He'd always had this bug about wanting to be a detective. He sure was smart. Maybe we didn't run much of a joke on him, after all. Chances are he didn't have no trouble studying it out."

"Who didn't have no trouble studying what out?" queried a voice behind him.

The two punchers turned to see Kurt Ridelle looking down at them with an inquiring smile.

"That fellow I used to work with down in Arizona," the Italian answered smoothly. "The one you mailed that birthday present to. Art's studying to be a detective. George and me doped out a secret message and sent it on to him to give him some practice. You know that old hymn book that nester give George when he was trying to convert him from his wicked ways?"

Ridelle nodded, chuckling.

"Well, I didn't have nothing to send him, so I asked George for that hymn book. George and me put the code message in it. That's what we was laughing about just now."

"You're a pair of kids," Ridelle said contemptuously. "You never will grow up and Eckhart is hopeless." And he turned and walked away.

Latizzo's eyes followed him with a malignant gleam.

"Look here, Saff," Eckhart demanded. "What are you stringing me that way for?"

"Stringing you?" Latizzo glanced at him quickly. "What do you mean?"

"You know damned well what I mean," Eckhart returned, "You and I worked side by side at Charley's ranch for nearly three years. We've been pretty good pals. But I never heard you once speak of this Art."

"You never heard me say anything much about anybody, did you? I never even told you anything about my own life, long as we've chummed around, only that I come from Montana."

"Granted," Eckhart admitted. "That's exactly why this Art business sounds phony, Saff. That message you sent to New York was pretty thin. What's back of it?"

Latizzo's eyes scrutinized him closely. "I don't know what you're driving at."

"Oh yes, you do," Eckhart contradicted. "The whole business is too queer to be straight. You put on it that 'for old time's sake' and that would have looked all right if you had signed your own initials to it."

"I did sign mine." Latizzo's reply was curt.

"Yeh," Eckhart drawled. "*Backwards.* And why did you add the brand of the Iron Kettle ranch?"

"I told you at the time!" Latizzo retorted impatiently. "Just to make the whole thing confuse him as much as possible. What's the matter with you, George?"

"Nothing, Saff. But you listen to me a minute. You made a clever play, but I'm not dumb enough to swallow it whole.

"Your initials backward are the initials of the man who owns the Iron Kettle, Lew Sudler. The name you gave your friend was so very peculiar that I got suspicious about it. One day when I was riding fence down that way, I stopped and asked the nester if he had ever heard any such Italian words as *articulo mortis.* He recognized the words right away, and said they weren't Italian, but Latin. *In articulo mortis*—meaning, *at the point of death.* Saff—" Eckhart leaned toward

Latizzo, his tanned face grim. "What's wrong at the Iron Kettle?"

"I don't know, George." Latizzo abandoned all dissembling. "But something is."

"Who's this amateur detective friend of yours?"

"There ain't no such person. That's all bull. I was making a play to get word to an old friend of Sudler's in the east. Either I'm a rotten judge of men and Lew Sudler is a skunk that needs stringing to the nearest tree—or there is a whole nest of skunks pretty damn close and Sudler's the victim. So I sent that message to Sudler's old friend, in such a manner that it would bring him to the Iron Kettle hot foot."

"Well, for criminey's sake, why didn't you just write him a letter and be done with it?" demanded Eckhart.

"I didn't dare. Just figure this out, George. A few months ago Kurt writes me to come up and help him stand off these rustlers. You and me both came. The first week we was here I asked Kurt who was doing the rustling. He said it was Lew Sudler. Then the fence between the Iron Kettle and the Floating R is broken down and some of our cattle rambles onto Lew's land. They promptly gets shot. Of course, Kurt says Sudler done it.

"Kurt sent some of the boys to mend the fence where the steers broke through. When they come back Rainey told me the wires had been cut.

Things are quiet for a little bit, and then that little water hole next to Sudler's fence gets poisoned and another bunch of Kurt's steers dies from drinking it. Kurt sent me to fill up the water hole. After which he told me to go on to the Iron Kettle and warn Sudler that the next stunt he pulled there'd be a shooting bee. I wasn't at all slow about going. I didn't like the look of the crew there. A bunch of roughnecks and cutthroats. I asked for Sudler. They said he was in the house. I found him in there with a guy which said he was the new foreman; a big ugly looking bruiser with a flat nose and little green eyes. I told Sudler that Kurt had sent me about the water hole. He asked what water hole. I could see from his eyes that he didn't know nothing about it. I was pretty certain that somebody was framing Sudler. I wanted to give him a chance to slip me a word if there was anything I could do. I said I'd been suspicious for some time.

"He never turned a hair, but he got me, and he said, 'If you're suspicious, why don't you do a little figuring, Saff? Call in a detective, or the sheriff or somebody?' I beat it. But I knew he had meant to tell me that he was in a jockpot and I was to get help.

"Have you stopped to think how tight Kurt has kept us boys for the last month? Won't even let anybody go to town. His excuse is that he's shorthanded and can't spare none of us. He even takes the mail in, and he watches it darn close. Now, if the fuss is between Kurt and Lew, and Lew is square, who's the crook? Kurt, of course. And he'd be on the lookout for anything that would throw a monkey wrench into his plans. He ain't in it alone, he ain't got the guts. And who's the other fellow liable to be? Why are we shorthanded? Because Kurt lent some of his men to Pete Phirquist. Phirquist is the other nigger in the woodpile. Phirquist and Kurt are in something together, and they're trying to pull a shady deal on Lew Sudler, but there's no rustling about it.

"As soon as I was sure of it, I began to figure how to get word to some friend of Sudler's. And I thought of this Taight. He's come out to the Iron Kettle to see Lew every year for as long as I can remember. But I couldn't just write him a letter. Kurt knows Taight too. If I'd give him anything to mail addressed to Taight, he'd of ripped it open to see what was in it. And I'd have got mine and done no good.

"So I rigged up this yarn about this friend of mine that went to New York to be a detective."

"But what in hell are Phirquist and Ridelle up to?" Eckhart asked.

"Sudler is in solid with a big cattle syndicate in the east. Taight's president of it. Sudler's got a sure thing. Consider, if Kurt and Phirquist had the Iron Kettle, along with the land and cattle they've already got. With the syndicate to buy their stuff, they'd sure be sitting pretty. I think that's what they want. But to accomplish it—they've got to get rid of Sudler. He'd never sell. So they do the next best thing. They frame him, and when they get him right where they want him, so that they will seem in the right and him in the wrong, they'll pop him off. He ain't got any heirs, no folks at all. They'd pick up his ranch at the sheriff's sale for half what it's worth. Smooth business, what?"

"But suppose Taight don't get wise to that message?"

"I'm making it my business to find out, George. He ought to be at the Iron Kettle now. For if he thought Lew was in trouble, he'd come fanning. So I'm going to sneak over to the Iron Kettle tonight, as soon as it's dark. If I don't come back by morning, you beat it for the Iron Kettle, too."

"If you don't come back? What do you mean?" Eckhart asked, startled.

"If I find Taight there, I'll stick. If I stay there, you come. Damn it, I wish we had a cracking good gunman to horn in with us. There was a fellow down on Charley's ranch, just before you came—and this is no bull. I'd have given anything to have signed up with that boy, but he wouldn't have me. Never knew much about him. He came from Louisiana, and I reckon he went back there. I don't even remember what his last name was. We always called him Jay. But boy, he sure could shoot. He could handle a pair of forty-fives as pretty as anything I ever want to see."

"Didn't you ever hear anything of him anymore?" Eckhart inquired.

"Never did." Latizzo rose, stretched, and started for the barn.

Eckhart rose and also fell into step with him. "You ought to send out a call for this Malo Hombre fellow they talk so much about."

"Humph!" Latizzo snorted. "I'll bet that guy couldn't last two seconds in a real fight. Can I look for you over at the Iron Kettle tomorrow if I don't come back?"

"You sure can ask some fool questions," Eckhart answered shortly.

Chapter XVIII

THE FIRST GUN

It was well after dark when Latizzo approached down the road to the Iron Kettle buildings and got off his horse by the barn. The man with the flat nose and little green eyes came out of the barn carrying a lantern and flashed the light in Latizzo's face.

"What'll you have?" he grunted sourly.

"I want to see Sudler."

"All right, go on in and see him if you want to." The man grinned insolently, and his small greenish eyes glimmered in the faint glow from the lantern. "It's all the good it'll do you. But hurry up and get out." He disappeared abruptly into the barn.

Latizzo's eyes sparked. He hurried to the house, ascended the steps and rapped on the rear door.

A man opened the door to him, a young man very near his own age, whose hard brown face was not too clearly seen against the light. Two heavy guns were slung about his waist, and in his dark eyes, glowing out of the shadows the night cast upon his features, was a shine like starlight on ice. The face and figure seemed oddly familiar to Latizzo.

"What will you have?"

"I'd like to see Sudler." Latizzo's black eyes moved swiftly over the outline of the poised powerful figure. Where had he seen the man before? The man stepped back and gestured for Latizzo to enter. The light fell full upon his walnut-brown face. Latizzo started, exclaimed in delight and held out a hand. "Jay! You old son of a gun! Where in hell did you come from?"

Instant recognition warmed the red-brown eyes, and a lean hard hand was thrust out to grasp Latizzo's. "Saff! You're the last person I'd ever expect to see here. Only got here today myself, just a few hours ago. But if you want to see Lew, come on in."

He closed the kitchen door, and Latizzo followed him into the bedroom. He had found Jay again! His eyes widened in surprise as he saw Sudler lying on the bed. Then his gaze flew across the bed. There sat Bruce Taight. Latizzo had little time to wonder about the presence of the bearded man standing by the foot of the bed, and the yellow-haired girl sitting by Taight. He heard Jay introducing him.

"People, this is Mr Latizzo, from—say, where are you from, Saff?"

"I'm at the Floating R, Jay. Came up there a few months ago to work for my old boss, Kurt Ridelle."

If that intelligence startled Malo, no one saw it. He nodded, and gestured toward Taight. "Let me make you acquainted with Mr Taight, from New York. Mr Costa and Miss Taight, accompanying Mr Taight."

Latizzo nodded acknowledgment, but he spoke to Sudler.

"Sudler, that day I was here, you realized that I was trying to make you understand that I thought they were framing you, didn't you? And you meant I was to get help? I was sure you did. So I sent for Mr Taight." Taight exclaimed in surprise, and the bearded man Jay had called Costa turned expressionless eyes on the little Italian. Latizzo turned to Taight. "You don't remember me, do you, Mr Taight? I've seen you, many times, when you used to come out to visit Sudler years ago. I was on the Floating R then. Don't you remember Saff?"

"Why yes, I believe I do remember you now," Taight replied. "But what do you mean by saying you sent for me? The book with the pin holes in it—*you* sent it?"

"I sure did." Latizzo launched into a swift summary of the chain of incidents which had preceded his sending the message. "Hasn't Lew told you nothing at all?"

"No. He's been hurt, and he can't talk. Somebody hit him on the head. He's temporarily paralyzed and can't even make signs."

"Huh! I knowed something bad was in the wind. Listen here." And Latizzo recounted to them the deductions he had detailed to George Eckhart. "Something's going to break soon. What we've got to figure most is on numbers—and guns."

"From what I've heard of him, Malo there is good as half a dozen when it comes to handling guns," Taight suggested humorously.

"Malo?" Latizzo frowned, and whirled to the man he had wished for with such vehemence. "Sure, I remember now. *That's* your name, Jay, ain't it? By all that's Holy, Jay, you ain't the Malo Hombre! Are you?" Malo merely grinned. Latizzo let out a whoop of delight. "I might have knowed it was you! Hell! But we need plenty, at that. Phirquist has twenty-six men, outside of himself and his foreman. That friend of mine on the Floating R, George Eckhart, will be here tomorrow."

"Just wait a minute, Saff," Malo cut in. "Your conjecture of what Kurt and Phirquist are trying to do is only conjecture. There are things we must know. What became of Lew's men? Who hit Lew on the head?"

The outer door suddenly opened and shut, and the huge man with the flat nose stood facing them. He had stepped inside, closed the door quickly, and now stood leaning against it. He addressed Malo belligerently.

"I guess it's about time to tell you guys that you'd better be quiet and not start anything unless you want to get hurt. None of you can leave the ranch. Don't even try to leave the house."

Malo tensed. He turned slowly until he faced the threatening figure against the door. Behind him he heard Cynara cry out, a small frightened cry. That was the devil of it, he thought in sharp irritation, women around. Why in the name of hell did Taight have to bring a woman? And especially a yellow-haired one! He did not speak. He merely stood watching the fellow warily, his hands motionless near his hips.

The man jerked the door open, walked out and slammed it after him. Tense silence succeeded his exit. Into the silence a sound rasped, a sound from Lew Sudler's powerless throat. Malo whirled around, stepped close to the bed and leaned over him.

He saw that Sudler was trying to point after the man who had just quitted the room. "Yes? What about him? If you could only communicate in some way. If you could only write. Couldn't you try, if I support your hand?"

Sudler closed his eyes in the agreed signal of affirmative. Malo got paper and pencil and sat down at the head of the bed, where he could conveniently reach and steady Lew's hand. The injured man made a colossal attempt to inscribe a legible message with the pencil. There developed only a rambling scrawl. Malo studied it, while Costa and Latizzo, over his shoulders, strove to decipher it. Out of the scrawl only a few letters were readable.

It was hi hit—that was all. After a moment's study, Costa pointed to the scrawl following the letters *hi.* "That looks like an M. Which would make it read—*it was him hit.*" His gaze flashed to Sudler. "Do you mean it was he who hit you on the head?"

Sudler closed his eyes and opened them eagerly again. A veritable cross fire of puzzled conversation flew about Sudler's bed. Both Costa and Malo questioned him concerning things which gave opportunity for more intelligent questioning since Latizzo had come and told what he knew.

The questions and answers revealed the fact that Sudler knew nothing at all of Pete Phirquist. Had never even heard of him. He had received from Ridelle no offer to buy the Iron Kettle, not even the hint of such an offer. He did not believe that Ridelle and Phirquist wanted to obtain possession of the Iron Kettle. There was something he did believe, something he wanted badly to impart. They knew that from the strained look in his eyes. But none of them asked the right question, and he could neither speak nor write. Finally Costa gave abrupt orders to let him alone, lest his condition be aggravated.

Malo rose from the bed and drew Latizzo aside. "You're right, Saff," he said in an undertone, intended only for Latizzo's ears. "We need numbers. What's going on here is no penny ante business. And we're a handful against a gang. I'm going after Dolf Kubik and his men."

"Who's Dolf Kubik?" Latizzo interrupted.

"Owner of the Cross Eight. He has nine men, ten counting himself. Your friend George Eckhart may not get here. We can count only on what we have right in the house. That's four. With Dolf's outfit, we'll be fourteen. That's none too many. Saff, you're on guard. All of you sit tight till I come back. I'll be here by tomorrow night at the latest."

He walked on toward the outer door, and half way across the kitchen he heard a cry behind him that halted his feet and drew his glance backward. It had come from Cynara. Her frightened grey eyes were intent upon him, her face was blanched. There was nothing surprising in her terror. Anyone could recognize the danger of their situation. But Malo's astonished senses told him that that cry and the look on her face were not entirely born of fear for herself and the others in the room who were her friends. Unmistakably he discerned a startled concern for himself.

Wondering, he went on. He reached the door, grasped its knob, turned the knob and threw the door wide. The big man with the flat nose stood there, half facing the door, an evil grin lifting his coarse mouth.

"Right on the job, bozo," he greeted Malo. The little green eyes leered. "Get back inside and mind your own business."

Two heavy guns leaped out of their holsters into the grip of brown fingers, their menacing bores trained on the big man with the flat nose.

"Step inside," Malo commanded, his voice low and curt. "And don't delay."

The big man scowled, then laughed contemptuously. But he entered the room, with his hands half raised in the air.

"Saff! Take this guy's guns and tie him up." Malo kicked the door shut with his heel, and Latizzo came on the run.

The captive cursed in rage, but he stood passive as Latizzo disarmed him and dropped the guns into Sudler's old trunk standing against the wall. He tied the man's wrists securely, and ordered him to lie flat on the floor while he bound his feet and gagged him.

"Hide him somewhere," Malo directed. "About the surest place to conceal him is under Sudler's bed. If anyone comes in looking for him, you can say that he and I went out together and you haven't seen either of us since. But for God's sake, Saff, hold down that temper of yours. Don't shoot, no matter what the provocation, unless it's a question of saving somebody else from a bullet. See you later." Again he started toward the door.

And again he heard the voice of the yellow-haired woman.

"Mr Malo!" She stammered, hesitated, then her voice rose. "Be careful. What would we do here if you didn't come back?"

Malo's hand was on the doorknob. He turned his head and glanced over his shoulder at Cynara. "I'll come back," he said, and passed out the door.

Chapter XIX

THE MAN OF LEGEND

He stepped from the house into the night, closed the door behind him quickly, and stood listening. In the faint moonlight all objects presented to his sight mere gradations and undulations of shadow. He started for the barn with a swift stride. No one intercepted him. He saw no sign of anyone about.

He entered the barn and felt his way to Pilgrim's stall. He saddled and bridled the big brown gelding, led the horse from the barn, and eased himself into the saddle cautiously. As he drew abreast of the end wall of the barn, a man stepped out to confront him.

The man himself was only a dense shadow. In his hand he carried a blind lantern. The tin guard around the chimney was turned toward him, preventing all light from the flame from shining in his direction. The small square opening in the guard sent a finger of light along the ground in front of the man who carried the lantern.

"Where you goin', Keene?" he asked in a low tone. He flashed the finger of light into Malo's face, spitting out an exclamation of startled surprise. "Oh, it's you is it? Where do you think you're goin'? Where's Keene?"

Keene, Malo deduced quickly, must be the man with the flat nose. He answered with curt brevity; "He's in front of the house, waiting for me. Keep out of this." But the man with the lantern leaped in front of him and caught the reins.

"You're not going any further till Keene tells me it's all right," he snapped. "Orders are not to let *anybody* leave the ranch."

Malo's right hand flashed to his hip, his right-hand gun rose in a swift arc and descended, the barrel crashing on the man's head. The fellow swayed, staggered and dropped. The lantern fell beside him, the streak of light falling across his figure, and Malo, in passing, saw only that he wore a red shirt.

At a cautious walk Malo rode Pilgrim past the house. Behind him rose a whistle, a signal from some other guard who had heard the horse's hoof beats. But now he had reached the gate and saw that it was open. He leaned low on Pilgrim's neck and gave the gelding his head. As he flashed beyond the gate and into the road, a gun barked from the direction of the house.

Inside the house Cynara, shaken and afraid, sat in a chair by Bruce Taight. Her eyes, widened and darkened, stared trance-like at the mute door beyond which Malo had disappeared. None of them spoke. They waited, all of them, tense, their ears strained for the least sound from outside.

Suddenly the silence of the night was shattered by the report of a gun from the front of the house. Cynara leaped to her feet, quivering, and cried out to Taight;

"Dad! They've shot him!"

Taight looked at her queerly. There was a note in her voice he had never heard before. A note that had never been there before. It appealed to him for denial. He rose quickly, placed an arm across her shoulder, listening intently.

Outside there rose the drumming sound of a galloping horse's feet, magnified in the silence of the night. It broke forth like a roll of bass thunder, diminishing and ebbing swiftly to a fading tattoo. Taight's grip tightened on Cynara's shoulder.

"The horse didn't stop. He's on his way." The forced quietness of his voice was intended to reassure her and steady her.

Her gaze raised to him, and she saw in Taight's eyes a penetrating and shrewd understanding of the unprecedented emotion that had forced that cry from her lips. Slow color drove the whiteness from her face. "I just—I—" she stammered, then forced herself into coherence. "I just don't want us to be cut off altogether from help."

"Yes?" Taight's eyes probed hers, and he said softly; "Cynara, don't lie to me anymore."

The stamp of feet clattered on the porch, the door swung open and a man entered the room, holstering a still smoking gun. He looked about the room with suspicious eyes, his heavy face darkened with a scowl.

"Where's Keene?" he demanded. "Where did he go?"

"Oh. You mean the big fellow with the flat nose?" Latizzo asked. There was a wicked glitter in his eyes. "He went away just a few minutes ago with the Malo Hombre."

The man started violently. "The Malo Hombre? What are you talking about?"

"Didn't you know that that friend of Sudler who came here today was the Malo Hombre?" Latizzo said deliberately. "He came here to see Keene, and they just went away together."

The man stood motionless, and an evil grin drove away his frown. "Damned if that ain't a good one! The Malo Hombre throwin' in with us! I suppose it's all right, if he went away with Keene. But even at that it looks a little phony. We had orders that *nobody* was to go off the ranch. Don't any more of you come out of the house. Next time I shoot I'll be close enough to hit what I shoot at." He stalked out and slammed the door.

Latizzo gloated. "He shot at Jay, but he missed him. There ain't any bullet fast enough to catch that boy!"

But the man who had fired at Malo was not satisfied with what Latizzo had said. He crossed the porch and stopped short at a sudden thought.

The little black-eyed fellow had lied, and he should have known it if he had given it second thought. Only one horse had gone racing down the road. Only one man had left the ranch. That man was not Keene. Keene had orders not to go, and to shoot anybody else who tried to go.

There was something wrong here, and the man who had shot at Malo meant to find out what it was. He would go and ask Woods if he had seen Keene. He stepped from the porch and started briskly toward the barn. Before he had gone twenty feet he saw a streak of light on the ground, and knew it for the glow from Woods' blind lantern. But what was it doing on the ground? His stride broke into a run.

He arrived at the spot to find Woods lying in an unconscious heap. The lantern, half overturned, was leaning against his thigh and the chimney was black with soot where the twisting flame struck it on one side. With a savage curse of dismay, the man snatched the lantern and set it upright. Woods stirred and groaned. He looked up into the other man's face with a dazed frown.

"Did you get him, Dent?"

"No." Dent shook his head. "How in hell did he ever get by you?"

"He cracked me over the head with his gun," Woods snapped, sitting up and feeling of his head. "Damn the fellow. I wish I could place him. I've seen him somewhere before."

"Well," Dent scowled down at him. "You steady, now? Get up then, and come with me. We're going into the house and find out what became of Keene."

Woods struggled to his feet. As he and Dent reached the steps and began to ascend them, both men drew their guns. They stepped across the porch. Dent turned the knob, kicked the door open, and the two walked in covering the occupants of the room beyond with their guns. None of the men moved, but Cynara caught at Bruce's arm and smothered a cry of fright.

Dent gestured with his head toward Latizzo. "That little black-eyed guy there, Woods. Take his gun away from him and frisk the other two. Then we'll search the house for Keene."

The little Italian rebelled in fury at being disarmed, but reason told him that resistance would accomplish nothing in his favor, and was almost certain to result in disaster. Dent saw the defiance in his eyes, and swung his gun upon Cynara.

"You make one false move, bucko, and I shoot the girl," he snapped.

Latizzo whitened. He knew it was no idle threat. He stood like a stone while Woods took the gun from his holster and went on to Taight. Finding Taight minus a weapon, Woods advanced to Costa. The detective stood moveless and contemptuously looked on while Woods searched him and took a small ugly automatic from his pocket. As he turned back to give the weapons to Dent, a heavy thump sounded upon the floor, as though a man had struck the floor boards with his heels. It had come from under Sudler's bed.

Woods crossed to the bed, knelt and glanced under it, then turned to Dent with an exasperated oath. "Keep your gun on that jane, Dent. They've got Keene under here tied and gagged."

Woods thrust into his belt the guns he had taken from Latizzo and Costa, holstered his own gun, reached under the bed and aided Keene to roll out where they could get at his bonds. In short time the big man with the flat nose was freed and on his feet. Instantly he assumed his leadership.

"Just keep that bunch covered, Dent, till I get my guns. This smart little guy dropped them in that trunk over there." He retrieved his guns from Sudler's trunk and joined Woods and Dent. He addressed the prisoners in the room with blunt finality. "Now you, if any of you are hankerin' to see how you'd look in a wooden overcoat, just make one more move to try to get ahead of us. And you," he snapped at Latizzo, "You tried to get funny with Dent. I could hear fast enough. If you know what's good for you, you'll come clean with me. Who is that guy with the funny looking eyes that got away?"

"I told Dent the truth," Latizzo answered. "He's the Malo Hombre."

"That's it!" Woods laid a quick hand on Keene's arm. "That's who he is, all right. I knew I'd seen him before. I was with Ginsler and his gang when the Malo Hombre made him dig up for Tommy Patchard. I couldn't place him at first, but I've got it now."

Keene's face darkened. "Well, the boss said for none of us to leave this ranch, Dent. But that puts a different face on things. Malo has gone for men, you can bet on that. We'll beat him to it. You get your horse and beat it for Phirquist's ranch. Pass the word that the Malo Hombre is on the warpath, backing Sudler. Tell him to send some men as quick as they can get here." He turned a leering snarl on Latizzo. "And you, Mr Wise Guy, keep your fingers crossed if you want to keep walkin'. By the time your Malo Hombre gets back here we'll be ready for him."

The three went out, slamming the door viciously, leaving behind them a group of stunned and hopeless people. Cynara turned imploring eyes upon Latizzo.

"How far is it to the Cross Eight?"

Latizzo shook his head at her. He knew her thoughts. "It's forty-five miles," he answered slowly. "A good fifteen miles farther than it is to Phirquist's ranch. I know what you're thinking. But it can't be done. He's got thirty more miles to go than Dent has."

He paused, listening, and Cynara caught

her breath. For the second time that night, the prisoners in the ranch house heard the sound of a horse galloping away, carrying a rider on an urgent errand.

Chapter XX

A GATHERING OF MEN

Dawn was breaking over the Cross Eight ranch. Dolf Kubik woke with a start to realize that someone was knocking urgently upon his door. He sat up in bed, shook himself wide awake, and called;

"Who's there?"

From beyond the door a familiar voice answered, "It's Malo, Dolf."

Kubik leaped out of bed. The door flew open, and closed behind Malo.

"There's trouble on the Iron Kettle, Dolf. Everything's in a hell of a mess. Sudler's flat, paralyzed, been knocked on the head. His whole crew's disappeared, nobody knows where or how. There's a bunch of bad hombres riding herd on the place. Lew and some friends of his from the east—one of them's a woman—are held prisoners in the ranch house."

"Wait till I get my boots on," Kubik interrupted. "You go rout out the cook and tell him to start some coffee going."

Malo vanished through the doorway. For the next half hour the Cross Eight ranch was a scene of bustling action. Men were saddling horses, oiling guns and stuffing belts with extra ammunition. Just forty-seven minutes from the time when Malo knocked on Kubik's door, eleven men rode away from the Cross Eight ranch headed for the Iron Kettle. Malo had asked one of the boys to ride to Dry Rock for the sheriff and a posse, and the grizzled old cook had interrupted indignantly;

"Say, what you think I am, anyway? One of these here passay guys? I can still fork a bronc myself. You boys all beat it for the Iron Kettle. I'll go to Dry Rock for the sheriff."

After they had heard Dent ride away that night, the five prisoners in the ranch banded together to fight despair. Latizzo seated on the floor against the wall, fell asleep with his head bowed upon his doubled knees, Taight dozed in his chair and Cynara's head dropped on his shoulder in slumber. Costa was the last to fall asleep. He had seated himself on the foot of the bed, and had been intently watching the injured man. Once he saw Sudler's hand quiver slightly, and he bent toward him. The motion was involuntary. The paralysis was beginning to pass. Another day or two and Sudler would be able to speak. Would it be too late? Costa finally lay down across the foot of the bed. The last thing he remembered before sleep overtook him was that Sudler's foot had made a faint move against his arm.

They all were abruptly wakened by the approach of a running horse. Latizzo sprang to his feet, stretched his cramped muscles and hurried to the window. Costa sat up on the bed, and Taight roused in his chair. Cynara got up quickly and followed Latizzo to the window.

"Is it—who is it?"

"It isn't Malo," Latizzo answered her double question, and gestured toward the barn.

The arrival was Dent. He was just getting off his horse, and Keene had emerged from the barn to speak to him. Latizzo turned from the window.

"If you aren't tired out, Miss Taight, we'd better get ourselves some breakfast. We're not licked yet."

Cynara's only reply was to square her shoulders unconsciously, and hurry toward the kitchen. The better part of an hour was passed in the preparing and consuming of a substantial breakfast. The girl and the little Italian had returned to the bedroom, and Cynara was feeding Sudler a cup of coffee with a spoon, when they heard the approach of other horses. Latizzo and Taight went to the window, and Cynara's questioning eyes followed them.

"Who is it?"

Latizzo turned his head to look at her.

"It isn't Malo. I told you it couldn't be done. It's the fellows Dent went after, three of them. And a harder looking crew I never saw."

Cynara advanced to the window, to look through the dusty pane. The three men had dismounted close to the house. Dent and Keene had joined them. They were three of a kind. Their faces were weathered and seamed, harsh and formidable. Two of them wore two guns. The other wore one revolver and carried a high-power rifle across the crook of his arm. His hair was jet black. His eyes matched it, and the short beard on his swarthy face was greyed slightly on the jaw. He spoke with the air of a man not in the habit of wasting words. "That Malo Hombre guy showed up yet?"

"No," Keene replied. "When he does, he's going to run into something he ain't looking for."

"You said a mouthful!" The dark man agreed. "Who've we got here?" Keene rapidly named half a dozen men, and the black-bearded fellow nodded. He asked how many there were in the house. Dent told him. He nodded again. "All right. We'll go in there and keep them company. When that guy shows up we'll have a nice little surprise party waiting for him."

Cynara bit her lip and whirled away from the window.

The three men came stamping across the porch and into the kitchen. One of the others closed the door behind them, and the black-bearded man walked part way across the room to dart a swift glance of scrutiny through the connecting doorway. He made some remark in a low aside, too low for those in the other room to catch what he said. The two men with him went over to the kitchen table, sat down by it in chairs that were handy, and kept their faces toward the other room. The black-bearded man walked about the kitchen, glancing idly here and there, until he caught sight of an old deck of cards lying on a window sill. He picked up the cards, walked back to his companions and tossed the deck upon the table.

"Deal 'em out, boys, and we'll kill a little time."

The next hour in that house was an endless nightmare for Cynara. When she could stand the silence no longer she would converse with Bruce Taight in strained whispers, and then lapse into silence again. She saw Costa frequently bend over Sudler, heard him speak to Sudler and heard Sudler strive to reply. Latizzo paced back and forth between the bed and the window, waiting in suspense for the first sound that would tell him Malo was coming. From the room beyond there came at intervals the low voice of the gunmen interchanging terse remarks, the slap of cards upon the table.

In that hour Cynara came to understand the pure relativity of time. They had been at the Iron Kettle three days. In those three days all the years before had been dwarfed. Yesterday a strange man had entered the house, and had assumed more importance than all the rest of the world. The twenty-four years she had lived in the east had been compressed into a brief period of initiation and tuition. The short hours, less than a day, since Malo had first walked through the doorway, were expanded into an eternity of living. Before he came she had been frightened numb at the threat of violence in the air. Now she was quivering and tense in every nerve, fiercely on the defensive for the man with strangely glowing eyes.

Suddenly a medley of sounds shattered the stillness outside the house. A startled shout from Keene, and the thundering hoofs of many horses, a shot from the barn and the answering roar of a dozen guns. With a half choked despairing cry, Cynara ran to the front window. Taight, Latizzo and Costa leaped to follow and crowd around her. Lew Sudler's frantic eyes strained after them. The three men at the table continued quietly to play cards, as oblivious to the racket outside as though they had not heard it.

Keene had leaped from the porch as the horsemen swept into view. At the sound of the approaching hoof beats, his warning shout had called seven men to join him. With Woods in the lead, they came piling out of the bunkhouse. Keene had whipped up his gun the moment he saw Malo sweep into sight with a string of men flanking him on either side.

Malo, Kubik, and the Cross Eight men poured a volley toward the eight darting to cover behind trees and at the corners of the ranch house. A bullet tore through the calf of Woods' leg as he darted behind a tree. A bullet from Keene's gun pierced the crown of Malo's hat, and jarred it like a passing breeze. In a concerted movement, Malo and the Cross Eight outfit vaulted from their horses and began to close in.

Keene had concealed himself around a corner of the porch. Kubik, in leaving his horse, for an instant came within Keene's range of fire. As the big man with the flat nose sent a bullet crashing toward Kubik, Malo threw down on him. Kubik staggered and dropped, desperately wounded, and Keene swayed and toppled. Malo's bullet had gone tearing through his brain. For a split second he had showed the top of his head. It had been enough.

The men behind the trees directed a vicious answering fire at the attackers. A rattling roll of a volley poured in from Kubik's men as they closed savagely. That volley took toll in earnest. Woods' gun dropped as a bullet cut into his forearm. The man beyond him grunted and slumped to a heap as a ball struck him in the stomach. Dent was not a fool. Keene was killed. Further resistance would result in slaughter. He threw both hands high, dropped his gun, and deliberately stepped into the open.

"All right, hombres," he shouted. "That's enough."

"Step out and line up then, all of you," Malo ordered. "Drop your guns damned quick."

There was a peculiar little gleam in Dent's eyes, malicious and triumphant. The Cross Eight men would approach the house off guard, believing themselves in command. The three gunmen, safe under cover, would mow them down like rats. Dent had saved the men he had left, to join the gunmen when the Cross Eight men had been slaughtered.

Malo gestured toward Woods and the man who was wounded in the stomach. "Crossby, you and Allen take those wounded men out to the bunkhouse. There is a doctor in the house, and I'll send him out shortly. The rest of you boys take these five fellows out to the barn and tie them up. I'm going to take Dolf in to the Doctor."

Inside Sudler's room the stunned group had stood at the window held motionless in fascination and suspense by what was taking place outside. As Malo started toward the house with Kubik in his arms, Taight, Costa and Latizzo moved aside. Cynara pushed between them with a gasp, her grey eyes blazing in her white face. As she heard Malo's step upon the porch, she saw the three gunmen in the next room rise to their feet, their hands at their holsters. She gripped Taight's arm, and her voice rose in a frantic whisper;

"Dad! They'll slaughter him!"

One of the gunmen whirled, whipped up his revolver and covered them. "Keep still! Not a sound out of you!" He commanded in a savage undertone. "One peep out of you and we'll drill the whole bunch."

Malo had not crossed the porch, and he kicked lightly against the door. They heard his voice calling; "Saff! Open the door."

The black-bearded man had turned his back upon the group in the bedroom, stepped to the door and opened it wide, then stood back and waited, his right hand on the butt of the gun in the holster at his waist. Malo stepped into the kitchen, and glanced in surprise at the three waiting him with drawn guns. His gaze centered on the face of the man with black beard, and the glow in his red-brown eyes warmed and flared.

"Well, I'll be damned! Wande!" He exclaimed. "Where did you come from? Is everybody in the country rounding up at the Iron Kettle?"

"It's him!" The black-bearded man exulted, turning to his comrades. "Lay off the guns, boys. It's him!"

The group in the room beyond stood spellbound and dumfounded. Malo crossed the kitchen and paused by the open doorway. "Will you come into the next room, Doctor Costa? I have another patient for you."

He carried Kubik into the front room which also opened off the kitchen. Wande, Coulone and Siletz trooped at his heels. Costa came out of the bedroom and joined them, with Latizzo hurrying to keep in step. Taight and Cynara followed only as far as the door. Malo paused by a low old fashioned box couch and laid Kubik gently down. The men stood back as Costa hurried up to bend over the wounded rancher. Malo, seeing Taight and Cynara standing in the doorway, took a step toward them.

"How's Lew?" he asked anxiously.

"Gaining slowly," Taight informed him. "He can move a little, and a while ago he managed to speak your name clearly enough for us to understand it."

Malo exclaimed in relief, and turned his attention to Wande. "How did you fellows ever get here?" he asked.

"Coulone and Siletz and me decided to try your way. We drifted into Arizona and took to punchin' cows, hopin' we'd run into you. We heard you say you come from Arizona. We finally rambled around to Wyoming and hired out to Phirquist's foreman for a job on his ranch up here."

"Yes, but what brought you to the Iron Kettle?"

"Phirquist said Sudler was heading a big rustling scheme, and he sent Keene and this bunch over here to keep Sudler out of mischief. We heard about the Malo Hombre, and wondered if it could be you. Dent came tearing in last night and said the Malo Hombre was on the rampage, backing Sudler. We didn't tell nobody. We just came ourselves. We knew if you was the Malo Hombre backing Sudler, then the crookedness was on Phirquist's side. And we're done with crookedness. That's all there is to it."

"No, there's plenty to come," Malo contradicted grimly. Then he saw Costa straighten and turn from the improvised bed. "What's the verdict, Doctor Costa?"

"He's very badly injured," Costa replied. "His chances are about fifty-fifty. I'll do all I can." His eyes lingered on Malo's browned features as he passed by and went into the other room for his instruments.

He returned in incredibly short time, divested of his coat, his shirt sleeves rolled to his elbows, with an instrument case in one hand. Cynara came behind him, bearing a basin of steaming water and some strips of torn white cloth. Her face had little more color than the cloth.

She followed Costa to the bed-couch, and Malo's eyes followed her. She was of tougher fiber than he had thought. He was compelled to respect her for her grit in a trying situation. There was a new light in the red-brown eyes as they rested on her yellow hair. Come to think of it, it wasn't just ordinary yellow hair. The pale shining waves were like—like ripe corn in the moonlight.

With a last glance at Kubik's unconscious face, Malo beckoned Wande and the other men from the room. They followed him into the bedroom, where Taight stood by Sudler. He paused by the bed.

"Lew, these three fellows here," he gestured toward Wande and Siletz and Coulone, "are old friends of mine, and darned good men to have in a pinch." He turned to Wande. "Spill everything, Wande."

"Well, we ain't seen nothin' that looks crooked about Phirquist at all," Wande replied. "What he said about Sudler sounded on the level. But if you're Sudler's friend, it can't be."

"What did he say about Sudler?"

"Well, he said Sudler was tryin' to rustle his cattle," Wande returned bluntly. "And he told us that Sudler had shot and poisoned some of Ridelle's cattle, over to the Floating R. He said Sudler was a old rancher in this country, and he'd have a hard time of it making the rest of the ranchers around here realize that Sudler was crooked as a snake. I don't see how Phirquist is doing anything crooked. He can't afford it. He works in too big a fashion. He don't dabble with no little stuff."

"Phirquist operates a little different from ordinary cattlemen. He buys a whopping big herd of cattle in the fall, winters them and sells them on contract in the spring. Ridelle helps him whenever he can, and Phirquist pays him a percentage. When we got up here to the ranch, the foreman showed us the cattle Phirquist had bought, and we started out with the roundup wagon. There was six thousand head, and we sure have been busy."

Malo studied a moment, then asked abruptly. "What have you boys been doing with the stock?"

"Just clarifying the brand," Wande explained.

"Well, something is sure rotten, Wande. Phirquist is a liar. Lew never rustled anybody's stock. And he never poisoned or shot Ridelle's cattle."

Sudler said, hoarsely, but quite intelligently;

"Jay!"

The frantic desire to impart something was apparent in his burning eyes. Again he strove to speak, and that frantic desire aided him to achieve a mutter that was barely intelligible.

"The—cat—tle."

"The cattle?" Malo repeated. "The cattle Phirquist bought?" Sudler managed a faint nod, and pointed a finger at Taight.

"Say—listen!" It was Latizzo's voice, rising excited and eager. "You're the president of a big cattle syndicate, Mr Taight. And your company's got a whopping big bunch of cattle running the range over beyond here, ain't it?" Taight nodded corroboration.

Malo exclaimed sharply; “Mr Taight! Who keeps an eye on the syndicate cattle for you?”

“Lew does, of course.” Taight eyed him in amazement. “Why, what has got you boys so excited?”

Malo turned again to Sudler, the glow in his eyes risen to a flame. “Phirquist was rounding up those syndicate herds, wasn’t he, Lew?” Sudler’s nod was very positive. Malo straightened. “Whew! Now we’re getting somewhere. You didn’t sell any of those cattle, did you, Mr Taight?”

“No, of course not. They’re not for sale.” Taight stared in bewilderment. “What are you trying to get at, Malo? Why should Phirquist be rounding up the syndicate herds?”

“Why, he’s rustling them, man! Wande, what brand was on those cattle?”

“The Star Block,” Wande replied, beginning to get excited himself.

Taight cried out, across Sudler’s bed, his face reddened and convulsed with fury.

“My brand! *My* brand!”

“He’s rustled all the herds Wande says he pretends to have bought and sold.” Malo’s eyes were ice cold. “No wonder he’s been coining money. And of course it was Ridelle who tipped him off to the syndicate herds laying around up here ripe for him to pluck. When they found Sudler was wise to them, they planned to put him out of the way. So Ridelle cuts his own fence, shoots his own cattle and poisons his own spring, planning to lay it onto Lew, so he could shoot Lew at the first chance; the whole country would consider Ridelle the wronged man, and Phirquist would make a clean getaway." Malo stepped up to the detective-physician. "What about Kubik, Doctor?"

Costa gazed at him with queerly smouldering eyes. "The moment I see any change I will tell you."

"If you've done all you can for him, there are some wounded men in the bunkhouse who need your attention. I'll go along and help you. I want to talk to Phirquist's men, anyway. I'm going to find out what became of the punchers who were working on the Iron Kettle."

Chapter XXI

TWO MEN TALK

Once outside of the house, Malo paused to speak to the Cross Eight men on guard at the door.

"I want to take Dent over to the bunkhouse, Ansen. Loosen his feet."

Dent glared malevolently as Ansen removed the thongs from about his ankles. But he went to the bunkhouse without protest. Malo shoved him ahead and halted him at the foot of the bunk upon which Woods lay, moaning with the pain in his burning wounds. Costa stopped just inside the doorway, looking on with interest, curious to see what was going to take place.

"Now, you two, the game's up," Malo addressed Woods and Dent. "The three men you had in the house are old friends of mine, and they gave me the low down on the whole works. It's time for you to talk, and to talk fast."

"I'm telling nothing." Dent snapped. Woods merely moaned.

Malo stepped close to Dent. "I'm not bluffing when I say we know the whole scheme. We know that Phirquist is a rustler, and how he has been stealing big herds and selling them as his own. We know he stole this herd he has now, from the cattle syndicate with which Sudler deals, and how he planned to get rid of Sudler. You tell me what I want to know, or, by God, we'll take you out and string you up, like so many coyotes. Ready to talk?"

Dent growled. "What do you want to know?"

"I want to know what became of Sudler's men?"

Dent winced, hesitated, and glanced at Woods. Woods was white with terror. Dent paled, and lost some of his bravado. "We, another guy and me, forced the foreman of the Iron Kettle, at the point of a gun, to tell the men that Sudler had sold the ranch and to pay 'em off. They didn't have no idea everything wasn't on the level."

"What became of the foreman?" Malo demanded.

"Keene bumped him off, at Phirquist's orders. He knew too much."

"All right, the rest of you fellows stay put. The doc will look you over, while I take this fellow back to the barn, where he belongs. I'll return immediately to help you, Doctor."

For the next three quarters of an hour Malo aided Costa in dressing the wounds of the men in the bunkhouse.

"I believe it would be wise to bring the wounded into the house, into that other bedroom opening off the front room," Costa suggested as he and Malo left the bunkhouse. "I'd like to have all the patients close together. I'll have to keep a close eye on both Kubik and that fellow who's shot in the stomach."

"I'll have it done immediately," Malo replied. "I'll put the prisoners in the bunkhouse, with Kubik's men on guard at the bunkhouse and one on the porch."

"Why a guard on the porch?" Costa interrupted curiously.

"So he can carry food and water to the others. And the pump is on the back porch. I've got to economize on men."

"I thought you sent for the sheriff from the Cross Eight?"

"I did, but the sheriff can't get here before tomorrow afternoon. He'll bring seven or eight men. Even at that, we'll be about a dozen against the whole Phirquist and Ridelle outfit."

Costa went on into the house. Malo hurried to the barn, to give orders for the moving of the prisoners and the wounded. Then he too went into the house, to help Costa make ready for the wounded Kubik's men were bringing in. Just inside the door, he found Latizzo standing in the kitchen talking to a tall man with a strong square face and a short brush of drab brown hair.

"Here's George Eckhart, Jay," the little Italian greeted him eagerly. "He just rode in. George, this is that fellow I told you about that used to work on Charley's ranch, the one I said I wished was here. And he's the Malo Hombre. One on me, George."

"Glad to meet you, Eckhart," Malo's keen eyes warmed, liking the sight of Eckhart's face and blue eyes. "Every man we can get is an asset. Did you bring any news from the Floating R?"

"Not much." Eckhart answered. "But it may be of importance. Ridelle is wise to the fact that somebody else is wise to him. When Saff didn't come back last night, Ridelle came out to the bunkhouse to ask if I knew. I said he was watching the range. But when he didn't show up by morning, Kurt got suspicious. I told him I'd go get Saff. He ordered me back. I kept going and he took a shot at me. Missed."

"But suppose Phirquist gets leery, and sends one of his boys over to see if everything's all set here," Latizzo said, glancing from Eckhart to Malo in anxious apprehension.

"Let him send!" Malo answered curtly. "But reason will tell you that Phirquist and Ridelle, having become suspicious, will get those cattle out of here as fast as they can move."

"I agree with you." Eckhart spoke briskly. "Still, there's a chance that they may come down on the Iron Kettle in a bunch."

"If the Phirquist outfit tries to raid this ranch before the sheriff arrives, they'll get a hot reception. Make yourself at home, Eckhart. I'm going to be fairly busy for a while. See you boys later."

Chapter XXII

FOR CYNARA

Within six hours the Iron Kettle had become a grim and threatening place. Every possible defense had been thrown up to prevent surprise.

Sudler was gaining steadily, but there had come upon him a feverishness that did not please Costa. In Kubik there was still no change. It was getting along toward ten o'clock when the man who had been shot in the stomach died and was removed to the barn. Malo came in from outside, and drew Costa aside.

"You lie down here on the foot of Kubik's bed and sleep till daylight. I'll wake you then. If there's any change in Lew or Dolf, I'll wake you before. Don't argue with me, Costa. You'll be needed a damn sight worse tomorrow. Get some sleep."

Costa shrugged his shoulders and capitulated. He *was* weary. He lay down at the foot of the unconscious man and closed his eyes. Malo went into Sudler's room, where Cynara was sitting and talking to Taight. Brusquely he told them they must sleep, he would watch Sudler. Taight would have protested but Malo cut him short. Cynara obeyed the order without a word. Malo had already arranged with the rest of the men to change off and get what rest they could. In another thirty minutes the Iron Kettle was quiet, asleep with one eye open, ready to leap and defend itself at the first hint of danger.

Malo was moving noiselessly from Sudler's room to Kubik's, and back again. His thoughts, to his own exasperation, were mostly upon the yellow-haired woman, who slept on a pallet of blankets by Sudler's bed. It was forced upon him, to realize that Cynara drew him inexorably, as nothing had ever drawn him before. He fought it grimly, determinedly, almost angrily. But he couldn't stem the onrush of his own emotions. He had some four hours to think about it, as he paced the floor between the two sick rooms, and his eyes frequently fell upon her face.

She showed little sign of strain, save for faint shadows under the grey eyes. It was nearing dawn when Malo paused by Sudler's bed and stood looking down at her.

All the scorn and hardness he had built up in his heart against yellow-haired women went down before his emotions. She was no longer merely a yellow-haired woman. She was Cynara, with hair like ripe corn in the moonlight. He bent over and touched lightly one of her outflung hands. Then, with his eyes burning, he straightened, walked into the other room, and woke Costa.

He went outside into the early dawn, to confer

with Latizzo and Eckhart. By the time he had made the rounds of the boys, it was broad daylight. He and Latizzo went into the house to get together a breakfast for the men. Cynara was up, and already had the breakfast started. Latizzo took off his coat and busied himself beating up the pancakes. Cynara started out to the porch to get a dipperful of water for the coffee. Tillson, the Phirquist man who was allowed his liberty to serve the prisoners, at the same moment approached the porch to get water from the pump. Cynara had taken the dipper and started to fill it.

"Give us a drink, sister," Tillson said.

Malo, from inside the kitchen door, heard and stepped into the open doorway. "Get your own drink, and attend to your own business."

"She's got the dipper," Tillson retorted.

"Then wait till she gets through with it," Malo snapped.

Cynara turned and started to enter the kitchen. Tillson reached out a hand and grasped her wrist. "I'll take a drink now," he said with angry resentment.

Cynara tried to wrench her hand free, but the man's grip was like a vise, and she dashed the water into his face. He cursed furiously, and twisted her wrist as she jerked it from his grasp. Cynara cried out at the sharp pain, and her face whitened with fear and anger as she sprang back against the wall.

With a roar of rage Malo leaped across the porch and to the ground. Tillson doubled up his fists and threw himself into the fight with a sneer. He was bigger and heavier than Malo, but he was as so much straw against Malo's fury. Latizzo had darted to the door. Coulone from the corner of the house, and Eckhart, who had been crossing the yard, joined each other a few paces from the combatants. Malo's face gave no evidence of the fury within him, and his eyes were as expressionless as his features. The others watched, fascinated by the cold anger that battered Tillson to the ground. The man fell senseless as Malo's fist crashed on his jaw. Malo promptly rolled him over, lifted him in his arms, and turned to speak to Latizzo;

"Saff, will you take Cynara in to the Doctor and have him look at her wrist? I'm going to tie this hombre up in the bunkhouse where he belongs."

He took Tillson to the bunkhouse, and came out again. No one was in sight but Eckhart, and as he started for the house Eckhart halted him.

"Will you come out to the barn with me, Malo?" he asked quietly. "I should like to speak to you, where no one will overhear." Malo assented, and followed him. Inside the barn Eckhart paused and looked Malo squarely in the eyes. "You drubbed that fellow pretty severely, didn't you?"

"He's lucky I didn't kill him!" Malo's voice was cold with fury.

"Yes. I expect so." Eckhart's face was oddly set. "Listen. Suppose she had been your wife, Malo. If you could do that to a fellow who merely wrenched a woman's wrist, what would you do to a hound who crippled a woman you worshipped?"

Malo stared at him in dumfounded amazement. "I'd kill him!" he answered harshly.

"I believe you would." Eckhart agreed grimly. "I knew a man once. His name was the same as yours, though he spelled it different—Malleaux. He had a wife he worshipped. They had a son. After the boy was born she was an invalid. A doctor operated upon her, deliberately experimented on her and had the nerve to admit it. His experimenting crippled her. Malleaux went crazy. The doctor got scared and left the country. Malleaux followed him, caught him and killed him. The jury was sympathetic in the light of Malleaux's grief. He was sentenced to the penitentiary for twenty years. The doctor's name was Guido Costa."

Malo stood like a rock. The anger in his eyes died to a smouldering black fire. His hard brown face was as expressionless as a mask of wood. "Are you—are you telling me about my father?"

"Yes."

"He sent you?"

"In a way. He didn't want to see you until you knew about him. He wanted you to know the life he loved. No other life would ever be possible for him. Not the cities. There he would be shunned as a jailbird. What young man wants to welcome a father with the stamp of the penitentiary upon him? But—that you might receive him and become his companion in the life he loved for the rest of his days, was the far-fetched hope that kept him alive in the living death of a penitentiary."

"Mother used to say," Malo's voice cut in, hard and emotionless. "That good men were bad, and bad men were good. I know what she meant. She came out here, to get out of the limelight and escape the scandal?"

"Partly," Eckhart confirmed. "And partly to escape Costa's brother. That is he in the house, Earle Costa, doctoring your wounded. He swore to revenge his brother's death, by taking you, and by killing your father when he got out of the penitentiary. Fury and grief had turned Malleaux mad. The law was merciful, but Earle Costa could find no excuse for your father. Just as Malleaux could find no excuse for Guido Costa."

"And my name is Malleaux!" Malo said slowly. "I stumbled onto my own name."

"Yes. Stranger things have been."

"Do you know where I am to meet my father? I remember only that his hair and beard were bright red, and that his name was Gem."

"He got out of prison five years early on good behavior, a year after you left Jason. Jason wrote him a letter, quoting a letter of yours. In it you mentioned your affection for Safaro Latizzo. He didn't want you to lose anything you had ever loved. He had lost so much himself. So he followed you to Charley's ranch in Arizona, and struck up a friendship with Latizzo. He was trying to figure out some way to get Latizzo up here, when Ridelle wrote Saff to come back to the Floating R."

"But where is *he?*" Malo demanded.

Eckhart's face went white. "When he went to prison the hair and beard came off. The years faded the red to brown. They called him Gem. For the simple reason that his initials spelled the word. George Eckhart Malleaux."

Malo stood as motionless as the walls around him. Two words came from his stiff lips, a curse and a prayer; "By God!"

"Prison bird," Eckhart said, in agony. A sob shook him from chest to thigh, and bent his shoulders. Malo put an arm around him as gently as though he had been a child.

"That's a hell of a way to greet your son, Dad! Buck up! We've got a long time to scrap together yet. What's gone—is *gone!* Here's to the future!"

Chapter XXIII

THE GRIM REAPER

"Malo!" Costa's voice called from the kitchen door. It was a note demanding haste. "Will you come quickly? Mr Kubik is dying." Malo went toward the house on a run, his father at his heels, and he heard a swift request from the elder man as they reached the steps. "Keep it between you and me, Jay. Let me remain George Eckhart for the present."

Malo nodded as they dashed up the steps and into the house. In the front room they came to a halt by the bed-couch, to find Kubik partly conscious, looking about him with puzzled eyes.

"How are you, Dolf?" Malo's voice brought his wandering attention clear, and he smiled.

"Oh, there you are, Jay! Got nicked a little, didn't I? But I don't feel any pain. Say, Jay, lean down closer. Don't let Ellen find out I got hurt. She might worry. Soon as I'm up, I might go see her. You're sure—she won't turn me down?"

"Dolf." Malo laid a hand on the dying man's shoulder. "I'm sure. All you've got to do is say the word."

Kubik's eyes flashed wide, a light of happiness blazing in them. But it blazed only to fade.

The flush in his cheeks deepened, ebbed. He sighed in utter content. The staring eyes did not close. Malo bent closer, gazed at him for a long moment, raised to his height and turned away.

"He died happy," Costa said softly, his eyes boring into Malo's face. "Even if it was a lie, eh?"

Malo stared at him, passed him by, and turned his steps toward Sudler's room. Bruce and Cynara followed.

Sudler was moving restlessly, muttering unintelligible things in his throat. Malo gazed at him intently, then hurried to the other room to bring Costa. Costa laid a professional finger on Sudler's wrist, and glanced at the flushed face.

"He's been this way the last thirty minutes, Malo," Costa informed him. "I was going to tell you, when I saw that Kubik was sinking, and that pushed everything else into the background."

Malo looked down at Sudler. "He's worse, isn't he?"

"Yes. If he could talk clearly he'd be raving in delirium. The tissues were damaged by the blow on his head. Some infection has started at the point of damage, resulting in an inflammatory process of the meninges. In other words, meningeal infection—incipient meningitis. In lay terms, to make it clearer, he's on the verge of brain fever."

The sound of galloping horses and shouting voices from outside cut him short.

"It's the sheriff, Jay!" Latizzo called. "The sheriff and fourteen men."

Malo turned quickly to Costa. "Doctor, I've got to go. By this time Ridelle has warned Phirquist and they'll be making ready to leave the country. You and Mr Taight will have to guard the house. With the aid of Coulone and the Cross Eight man. The rest of us here have got to move."

Sudler's murmuring had increased. "Lew. Lew, don't you know me?" Malo put a hand on Sudler's shoulder and tried to draw his attention, but Sudler's gaze passed over him unseeing. Malo straightened and turned to Costa. "Doctor, give all you've got to Sudler. I'll be back as quick as I can get here." Costa gave him a faint nod, and as Malo turned away from the bed, he started from the room, and as he passed through the door he was aware of swift feet coming behind him. He stopped and turned his head, to look into frantic grey eyes.

"Please!" Cynara's voice quivered, stumbled despairing to a halt.

His eyes stared at her coldly, the more coldly because he held in with harsh repression the feelings within him. Once he had thought that he loved. Now he knew that he did. He stood as motionless as though nothing within him was moved, though every nerve of his body cried to him to take the woman in his arms. She saw nothing of the tumult, save that in the red-brown eyes the deep glow had flamed to a high possessive light.

"I'll come back." The words were so low she hardly caught them. "I'll always come back—where you are." And not even Cynara Taight ever realized what it cost him.

Chapter XXIV

RUSTLER'S PAY

Kurt Ridelle and Pete Phirquist were working like madmen, pushing their full combined crew to the limit of endurance.

The men had got together the roundup wagons and the horses, saddled their mounts and with Phirquist and Ridelle in the lead, started out, the roundup wagons trailing behind. They had passed out of sight of the ranch buildings, crossed the ridge of a hill and begun the descent on the other side, when Phirquist spied a dust cloud rising from the hoofs of oncoming horses. He spoke quickly to Ridelle.

"They're after us. Shove the boys back over the hill, quick!"

The men whirled their horses and raced back to recross the hilltop, and the heavy wagons turned to follow them.

From the shallow valley below, Malo and the sheriff had seen the scattering crew dash back over the hill, and had seen the lumbering wagons follow. The sheriff snapped swift orders. He split his band in two. The two bands parted and advanced around the hill, to close in and attack Phirquist's outfit at both ends of the line.

Over hill and valley the battle broke. The bluffs echoed back the detonations of guns that crashed like the rattle of infantry fire. Men cursed and shouted. Horses screamed and snorted in pain and terror. The hills were swept with the thunder of half a hundred guns. Ever more swiftly the rustlers gave ground, their numbers lessening rapidly. They saw Phirquist go down shot through. It was then that one of Phirquist's men saw the sheriff's star, and he cried out frantically to the others that they had been duped.

With both hands high, the puncher rode out and shouted a request that they be given a chance to surrender.

Malo paused to speak to the sheriff. "What's the next move, Sheriff?"

"Well, you've got a doctor over to the Iron Kettle. I guess we'll just take the whole bunch back there, and let the doctor see to these fellows; pile them into the roundup wagons."

"But what's it all about?" demanded the man who had asked to surrender. "Phirquist told us you were rustlers."

"Phirquist was the rustler himself," the sheriff answered briefly. "There'll be plenty of time for explanation when we get over to the Iron Kettle."

Chapter XXV

THE LAST CHAPTER

It was a grim train that came to the Iron Kettle at dusk. Phirquist's foreman, dying in one of the wagons, had willingly and wearily laid the whole rustling scheme bare. Only he and Ridelle, Dent and Keene, had been in Phirquist's confidence.

While Costa hurried from man to man, dressing wounds, Malo hastened into Sudler's room, Latizzo and Eckhart following him close. Cynara was sitting on a chair at Sudler's side, and Taight was pacing the floor in agitation. Sudler was muttering steadily, in jerky, painful sentences, numerous words that were clear but made no sense.

"He's worse!" Malo exclaimed sharply.

"Yes." Cynara shook her head sadly. "Earle says there isn't much chance."

Malo took a seat in a chair near Sudler, waiting in suspense till Costa should have finished with the wounded and come into the room. Sudler's restless babbling filled the room. Finally Costa came, and Malo sprang to his feet with an eager question. Costa waved him aside.

"Just a minute, Malo. Everybody else must get

out of here." When they were gone, Costa turned to Malo.

"I can't give you anything definite. He hasn't slept for days. He's growing steadily worse. There's only one chance for him. The whole thing depends on forcing him to relax and rest. Something is worrying him. Something of which I can get neither head or tail. I can't reach him. If we could straighten out his mind and get him quieted, it would be easy. Otherwise—there isn't any hope. You'd better go get some sleep yourself."

"No. I'm staying right here by Sudler. If I can't do anything else, I'll be with him till the last. Go on to your wounded, Doctor."

Costa gave him a long curious stare, something smouldering deep in his eyes, turned silently and quitted the room.

Malo reseated himself by the bed, alone with the man he had come so far to reach. And now Lew was going from him. If he only could tell what was bothering Lew's mind. He bent close to listen to the incessant muttering. Some of it was quite clear. Malo caught scattered sentences that made him grow rigid.

"You're all wrong." The muttering voice was impatient. "You can paint all you want to—in our house. Ellen—let the career go hang." The mutter sank to an unintelligible jumble, then rose in an incoherent plea. "Ellen—say you didn't mean it—it—you said you'd never sing it again—sing it—sing it for me now—and I'll know it's all right. Ellen—"

Malo listened, strained and tense, and the whole story was laid before him. Lew Sudler was the man Ellen Calleot had loved. It was Ellen Lew wanted now, groped to call in his hurt mind. Ellen, who lived with "Windbreak" because she could not forget. Swift realization leaped into the Malo Hombre's brain. He sprang to his feet and rushed out into the other room to find Costa. The detective-physician stood talking to Taight and Cynara. All three of them glanced up, startled, at Malo's haggard face and blazing eyes.

"Doctor, have you done all you can?"

"Why, certainly!"

"Will you deliver him over to me?"

Costa stared. "All I have to say is, if you can do anything to reach him, do it quick."

Malo whirled to Taight. "How fast can you drive with the big car of yours? How long will it take you to make ninety miles?"

Taight, tense and gripped with sharp interest, answered curtly; "Not long. How are the roads?"

"Like all the rest of the roads around here. No better, no worse—no bad hills."

"I should say around three hours. Why?"

"Get the car." Even as Malo turned to Costa again, Taight darted toward the outer door. "Six hours. Doctor, have we got six hours?"

"If we don't get him quieted, you have little more." Costa's eyes suddenly riveted on the grey flannel shirt Malo wore, on a spot below his arm. "There's blood on your shirt. You're hit! You can't go till I attend to that wound."

"It's only a scratch," Malo answered quickly, backing away. "You can take care of that when I return."

He turned his eyes on Cynara's white face. "You know what I told you—wherever *you* are!" He wheeled, dashed across the room and followed Taight.

The big car roared away from the Iron Kettle, on a race with death.

In two hours and a half it came to a halt before Ellen Calleot's house. She opened the door before Malo reached it.

"Mr Malo! What's wrong? What do you want?"

"I want you," Malo returned bluntly. "And I want 'Windbreak.' Lew Sudler is dying. Only one thing can save him—you. You've got to throw that pride to the winds and come with me."

Five and one half hours from the time of their departure, the big car rolled to a stop by the ranch house. Costa opened the door to them. Malo and Taight hurried in carrying the long pole over which the great picture was rolled. Ellen followed, and as Costa closed the door behind her, Malo spoke to him in a strained voice.

"I want your last word, Doctor."

"If you can quiet him in the next hour," Costa answered steadily. "If you can get him normally asleep, I'll answer for his recovery."

A wondering, hushed group watched from the connecting door as the strange thing that was done at Malo's orders. The great painting was carried into Sudler's room and stretched upon the wall beyond the head of Lew's bed. Malo took from his pocket a small object he had snatched from Ellen's window sill, and dashed something against the boards at the foot of the wall. A powerful pungent odor rose in the air. Ellen Calleot stood a little apart, waiting in white-faced suspense. Malo led her into the room and halted her by the bed. She looked down upon the face of the man who had loved her for twenty years.

Lew's voice rose in incessant babble. "Ellen—you said you never would. But sing it—now—and I'll know it's all right."

"That's what you've got to do," Malo said tensely.

"I can't!" Ellen's voice was a frantic whisper. "I haven't been able to sing for years. I can't."

Malo's jaw clamped. "Then go over there and stand by the painting."

She obeyed him dumbly. He slipped by her and passed out of sight beyond the head of the bed.

He had sung it once to help a man to die. He must sing it now to help a man to live.

> "You took the ring I gave you nor cast a glance at me
> As you held that jeweled trinket in your hand,
> Then you turned aside and cast it in the waters of the sea,
> And the waves were splashing idly on the sand."

The babbling voice faltered, hushed, and began babbling again. But words, old and familiar, began to reach the tired brain.

> "You turned away unheeding the tears I could not hide,
> You turned away and not a word was said.
> But my stubborn heart is breaking underneath its mask of pride—"

The twisting restless body on the bed lay still. The babbling voice trailed to silence. Sudler's head turned slightly, held rigid, listening.

> "I awake from bitter dreaming just to call aloud your name,
> I fall asleep to dream of you once more,

But my stubborn pride has left me, I
admit I was to blame.
Come back, dear, and love me as before."

Sudler's rigid head turned still further; his eyes, clearing fell upon Ellen Calleot. Malo had builded better than he knew. Lew Sudler saw the woman he loved standing by the eucalypti, by the windbreak where they had walked together. Twenty years were wiped away, were as if they had never been. He stared, and very slowly he raised himself to one elbow. Pungent odor came from the trees.

"Ellen!" His voice rose in a shout. "I've tried to find you for fifteen years."

Quietly Malo slipped from the room and closed the door behind him. Eckhart gripped his arm.

"Jay, you've got to come immediately and let Costa see to your side."

Malo made no resistance. He slumped, weary and exhausted, swaying on his feet. Between them, Latizzo and Eckhart aided him to walk into the front room, and laid him down on the box couch they had in his absence made ready for use. Costa bent over him, and Cynara stood close, her face as white as paper. Malo closed his eyes and set his jaw, while Costa made a swift examination. The physician rose to face Taight.

"The boy's got a bullet in his ribs. Cynara, no fainting or any of that kind of foolishness. Get me some water and cloths quick!"

Cynara drew herself together with a great effort, and went blindly from the room.

Costa spoke quickly. "The bullet's embedded in a rib. I've got to get it out before she gets back." He leaned to his instruments. He picked up a knife, with a long sharp blade, and suddenly became aware of the nose of a gun prodding him in the side. He turned his head to see Eckhart covering him, his face grim and white.

"Be careful," Eckhart said tonelessly. "Remember whom you're working on, Costa."

Costa glanced down at the gun, and then steadily up into Eckhart's face. "Listen. In my life I have learned many things. In the last two days I have learned twice as many. One of them is that revenge is a foolish thing. I knew you the minute you came into the house. I've seen this boy in action—and I know a man when I see one. You put down your gun, and I'll put down my knife. That is figurative, but you understand."

Eckhart's face quivered. The meaning was unmistakable. He thrust his gun back into its holster. With a quick motion Costa picked up another instrument, and bent again over Malo. When Cynara returned to the room, the bullet had been removed, and Costa was ready to cleanse and dress the wound. It was quickly done, and Latizzo could stay silent no longer.

He drew close to Malo. "Jay, I just got to know how you feel."

"I'm good as new, Saff."

"You can all get out of here," Costa ordered. "Cynara," and his glance lingered intently on the girl, "you may stay. And you, George—but the rest of you must go."

Wande, Siletz and Coulone joined Taight as he followed Latizzo out the door.

Malo opened his eyes and looked up into Cynara's face. He had to meet the last problem squarely. "Cynara, my father stands beside you there—George Eckhart Malleaux. He spent fifteen years in the penitentiary for murder: the murder of Guido Costa. But he's my father, and I'm proud of him. Would you marry an ordinary cowpuncher, who has nothing else to offer?"

Cynara caught her breath on a sob. She dropped on her knees by the couch, and buried her face upon his shoulder. He heard her whisper, muffled against his arm. "I—I'd marry—you." Malo reached out blindly with his other hand, to grip hers.

Malleaux, his face quivering, his eyes blurred, smiled down at his son and turned to leave the room. As he passed the couch Costa fell into step with him. But they both paused as they saw Ellen Calleot coming swiftly toward them from Sudler's room. Her face was transfigured. She said gently;

"He is asleep."

Center Point Large Print
600 Brooks Road / PO Box 1
Thorndike, ME 04986-0001 USA

(207) 568-3717

US & Canada:
1 800 929-9108
www.centerpointlargeprint.com